Treasure Island

P9-AOX-414

Robert Louis Stevenson's

TREASURE ISLAND

First published in 2006 by Usborne Publishing Ltd,
Usborne House, 83-85 Saffron Hill,
London EC1N 8RT, England.
www.usborne.com

A catalogue record for this title is available
from the British Library.

Printed in Great Britain

Series editor: Jane Chisholm
Designed by Tom Lalonde
Series designer: Mary Cartwright
Cover design by Zoe Wray
Cover image © Arthur Thévenart/CORBIS
background © Craig Aurness/CORBIS

TREASURE ISLAND

from the story by

Robert Louis Stevenson

retold by *Henry Brook*

Illustrated by *Ian McNee*

Contents

About Treasure Island

Robert Louis Stevenson was lounging in a rain-lashed Scottish cottage when he had his first ideas for the book that would make him famous: *Treasure Island*. Dreary weather had kept him and his family confined indoors for several days. So, to keep his young stepson entertained, Stevenson suggested they try some painting. One of their sketches was a map of a make-believe island. Stevenson joked that the isle was a pirates' den and he covered it with woods, swamps, crosses and other mysterious symbols. Working away at his picture, the writer's imagination suddenly sparked into life. *As I poured upon my map of Treasure Island,* he wrote later, *the future characters of the book began to appear there... among imaginary woods and unexpected quarters... the next thing I knew, I had some papers before me and was writing out a list of chapters.*

Stevenson was already well-respected for his travel books, essays and short stories. But, at the age of 30, he still hadn't completed a full-length novel. He'd made dozens of attempts, but always got distracted or bogged down in the complexities of a long story. But his treasure map gave him a strange new feeling of confidence. Stevenson started writing feverishly, determined to produce a pirate classic.

He wanted his book to be a pure adventure - *no fine writing or psychology*, as he put it. From the opening sentences, the reader is drawn into a murky, foggy world of roadside inns, wandering cut-throats and dangerous secrets. The sea is a constant murmur in the background, as though the island itself is calling to Jim Hawkins, the young hero of the story. To help create the ghostly, compelling atmosphere for his book, Stevenson borrowed unashamedly from earlier writers. Billy Bones, the rum-sodden ruffian who stalks Hawkins' inn, is similar to one of the characters dreamed up by Washington Irving, the author of *The Legend of Sleepy Hollow* and *Rip Van Winkle*. Stevenson admitted to borrowing other material from several sources, among them Defoe's *Robinson Crusoe* and a short story by Edgar Allen Poe. But he didn't simply copy other writers' ideas; he refined them and so made them his own. In the process, he created a character who must rank among the most famous in world literature: Long John Silver.

The original title of the book was *The Sea Cook*, in recognition of how central Silver is to the story. Although he doesn't appear until almost a third of the way into the novel, Silver's gruff, menacing figure haunts the dreams of Jim Hawkins from the first pages, after Billy Bones warns him to beware the one-legged man. The reader can always sense Silver prowling at the edge of the action. He was there when the treasure was robbed and buried - long before the story begins - and seems to be pulling all the strings both on board and on land. His smooth tongued patter, combined with physical might, allow him to cross the social boundary between officers and crew. Silver is a great literary creation, and, once encountered, almost impossible to forget.

Stevenson wrote a chapter a day, and read each new one to his family, gathered around the fireplace in the evenings. He was keen to test the pace and excitement of his story on Lloyd, his stepson, using him as a sample audience. But he soon discovered that his own father was equally gripped. The elderly man got so involved, he even proposed the list of items found in Billy Bones' chest, and insisted on the name *Walrus* for Flint's ship.

For fifteen days, Stevenson raced through his novel, but, on the morning of the sixteenth, he sat down and found he didn't have a word to say. Try as he might, he couldn't make any progress, and he began to despair that this book was going to collapse like all his other attempts. For several months, he turned his attention to other work, until one day he happened to pick up his pirate manuscript during a stay in the Swiss mountains. Once again, his pen flowed - and in two weeks he'd finished his first book. It was a publisher who suggested the new title - *Treasure Island* - and Stevenson happily agreed. He still believed that the entire story - with all its amazing characters - owed everything to his accidental sketch of a treasure map. That painting, on a bleak and rainy day in Scotland, ended with a book that has never been out of print and has sold millions of copies all over the world.

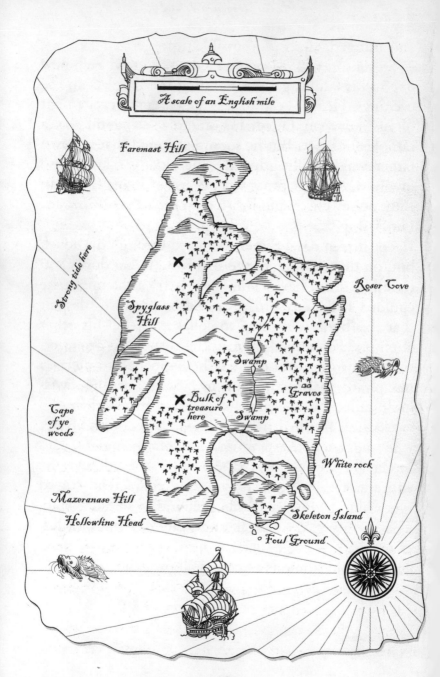

A Sailor Calls

Squire Trelawney, Doctor Livesey and the other survivors of the expedition have asked me to write a full account of our adventure on Treasure Island. They've told me to hold nothing back except the island's location, and to keep this secret only because there is more treasure buried in that cursed place. Nothing could persuade me to return to that island of terror, but perhaps my friends still dream of another voyage and further riches. So I begin, with the arrival of the old sailor at the inn my father owned, the Admiral Benbow, in a lonely bay on the English coast...

I remember the stranger as if it were yesterday. From my bedroom window I spotted a tall, thickset man plodding along the cliff path towards the inn. He was a sea dog, I guessed, sun-scorched and worn, with a greasy pigtail sprouting from under his peaked hat, trailing down a patched blue coat. As he came closer, I could see his huge hands, all ragged and scarred, the nails black with grime. A servant followed behind him, pushing a handcart loaded with an enormous, padlocked sea chest. But the stranger acted as though he was alone on the cliffs, whistling to himself and glancing around the cove. As he turned his head, I saw an old sword wound across his cheek, a livid white scar on his tanned skin.

Suddenly, he broke into a song, in a rasping voice broken by decades of storms and hard living at sea:

"Fifteen men on the dead man's chest -
Yo-ho-ho and a bottle of rum..."

He rapped on the door of the inn with the heavy stick he was carrying and bellowed: "Landlord, bring me rum."

My father hurried out with a bottle and glass and the seaman sipped his drink slowly, lingering on every drop like a connoisseur.

"I like this cove," he growled suddenly. "And I like your rum. Do you get much company round here?"

"Very little," replied my father, "the more's the pity."

"But that's just how I like it," said the seaman, with a leer. "This is the right berth for me."

He beckoned to his servant: "Take my chest in here, matey. I'm staying a while. Now, landlord," he continued, addressing my father, "I'm a plain man, with simple needs. All I want is rum, a bed, bacon and eggs, and that cliff up there to keep a lookout for ships. You can call me Captain, and take my rent out of these."

With a flick of his wrist he scattered a handful of gold coins across the threshold of the inn.

"Tell me when you want more," the man snarled, bringing himself up to his full, fearsome height. "Bring the chest," he shouted over his shoulder, snatching the bottle from my father and striding into our house.

Even with his shabby clothes and coarse speech, the seaman had the natural bearing of a commander. He was used to giving orders - and being obeyed. My father questioned the servant, but all he could learn about our new guest was that he'd arrived on a mail coach that morning, at a town further along the coast. He had asked around for a lonely inn, and when the *Admiral Benbow* was recommended, had hired the porter to transport his chest. The servant was running back to town as soon as the luggage was inside, glad to be free of his gruff master.

Our Captain was a silent man most of the time, who only wanted to be left alone. All day long he prowled the cliffs, peering out to sea through a brass telescope. In the evenings, he sat in a corner, sipping rum and glowering at anyone who dared to approach.

Each day, on his return from the clifftop, he asked if any sailors had passed by the inn. At first, we thought he was anxious to meet other nautical men.

But I soon learned that the opposite was true: he wished to avoid any contact with them. When a sailor did stop at the inn, the Captain always peered around the door to examine the visitor before entering the room. Until the new guest was on his way again, he crept around the inn, as silent as a mouse.

A few days after his arrival, the Captain decided to take me into his confidence. "Come here, boy," he hissed, as I was passing his table. "Would you like to earn yourself a silver coin, doing a little job for me?"

"Aye, sir," I answered. "Of course, sir."

"If you keep your weather-eye open," he whispered, "I'll give you a silver four-penny on the first of each month."

"But what am I to look for, sir?" I asked.

"A seafaring man," he answered. "An old tar with one leg. And, if you spy him, come running to me and let nothing stop you."

Often enough, when pay day came round, the Captain would blow through his nose and chuckle when I asked him for my money. He always gave in though, handing me a coin and repeating his instructions: "Watch for a seafaring man with one leg."

This one-legged man haunted my imagination and pursued me in awful nightmares. On stormy nights, when the wind shook the four corners of the inn and the breaking surf boomed around the cove, I saw him in a thousand different, hideous shapes. Sometimes, his leg was missing at the knee. In other dreams, it was cut off at the hip, or jutting from the middle of his torso, as though he were some kind of supernatural

beast. Whatever his shape, he was always chasing after me. These nightmares were a heavy price to pay for my monthly silver coin.

My fear of the one-legged man made me less afraid of the Captain, but he terrified our other guests. On nights when he'd had one rum too many, he would sing wicked sea songs that made the customers tremble. Sometimes, he would order drinks for the house, then force everyone to listen to one of his blood-chilling stories, or make them accompany him in a chorus of *Yo-ho-h-o, and a bottle of rum*. The whole inn shook with singing, as our regular customers joined in for dear life, afraid of annoying the Captain with a lack of enthusiasm. During these drunken spells, he was the most demanding companion, slamming his fist down on the oak table for silence, or flying into a rage if he was interrupted. Only when he staggered off to his room, drunk and sleepy, was his audience permitted to leave.

The Captain's stories frightened people more than anything else. He described hangings and men being made to walk the plank, tropical storms, pirate raids and massacres, all in the most elaborate and gruesome detail. If only a tiny part of what he said was true, he must have lived among the worst desperadoes and killers ever to set sail on the ocean. The language he used was so wild, some of the simple country folk covered their ears in shame.

My father feared our regular customers would be driven away by the Captain's bullying and blood-soaked yarn-spinning, and we'd be ruined. But I wasn't so sure. Secretly, I thought the local people liked to be shocked and scared, as their lives were so dull. Some of the younger men even pretended to admire our guest, calling him a *true salt* and the kind of man who made England feared and respected around the world.

Whether he repelled or attracted customers to the inn, the Captain certainly ruined us in other ways. He was mean to the point of avarice, endlessly repairing his tattered clothes until his coat looked like a patchwork quilt. His stay stretched from weeks to months and, although the deposit he'd given us was soon exhausted, my father was too timid to ask for more. When he dared to raise the subject, the Captain snorted through his nose so loudly, it sounded like a lion's roar, and fixed him with an ugly stare. The seaman became a terrible burden on my father's nerves, and surely contributed to his final illness.

It was after one of Dr. Livesey's visits to my bedridden father that I finally saw the old sea dog meet his match. The doctor had gone into the bar-room to smoke a pipe, while waiting for a groom to bring his horse. (We had no stabling at the *Admiral Benbow*, and it was a few minutes walk to the nearest hamlet.) I had noticed the striking contrast between the doctor, smartly dressed with a powdered wig as white as snow, and the plain country folk at the inn. But the greatest difference was with that filthy, scarecrow of a pirate, who was lounging at one of the tables, bleary with rum.

Suddenly, the Captain broke into song:

> *"Fifteen men on the dead man's chest -*
> *Yo-ho-ho, and a bottle of rum!*
> *Drink and the devil had done for the rest -*
> *Yo-ho-ho, and a bottle of rum!"*

When I had first heard these words, I imagined the chest must have been the same one he kept locked in his room, and the thought mingled with the one-legged man in my nightmares. I was so used to the tune by now, I ignored it, but I noticed that Dr. Livesey didn't like it one bit. He glanced up angrily from a conversation he was having. A moment later, the Captain slammed his fists on the table, giving the signal for silence. Every voice in the bar stopped at once, all except for Dr. Livesey's. Clearly and politely, he carried on talking.

The Captain glared at him for a while, and when this had no effect, beat the table with his gnarled fists. "Quiet there," he barked. "No talking between decks."

"Were you addressing me, sir?" asked the doctor.

With an oath, the Captain assured him he was.

"In that case," said the doctor calmly, "I have only one thing to say to you. Keep drinking your rum, and the world will soon be rid of a very dirty scoundrel indeed."

The old sea dog's fury was terrible. He jumped to his feet, snatched a sailor's knife from his pocket and flicked it open. "I'll pin you to the wall," he snarled.

"If you don't put that away this instant," replied the doctor steadily, "I promise, as a gentleman, that you shall hang for it."

Both men glowered at one another, but it was the Captain who backed down. He sheathed his knife and shuffled off to his table like a whipped dog.

"Since I now know there's a man like you in my district," added the doctor, "I'll keep an eye on you day and night. I'm a magistrate, you know, and if I hear a whisper of a complaint, I'll have you hunted down and sent packing. I hope that's clear."

In a moment, the groom arrived with the doctor's horse and Livesey rode away. The Captain was quiet for the rest of that evening, as he was for many evenings to come.

Black Dog

Not long after this, we had the first of the mysterious visitors who would finally free us of the Captain, while dragging us deeper into his affairs. It had been a bitterly cold winter, with hard frosts and heavy gales lashing the coast. Nobody expected my poor, sick father to see the spring. He was confined to his bed, leaving my mother and me so busy running the inn, we paid little attention to our unwelcome guest.

It was early one January morning, when the frost was glistening around the cove and the sun was still low in the sky, that I heard the Captain shuffling about in his room. As he left the inn, I stepped over to my window to see what he was up to. He was making for the beach, his cutlass swinging under the broad skirts of his old, blue coat and the brass telescope glinting under one arm. It was so cold, his breath hung in the air like wreaths of smoke, and I thought I could hear him snorting in a rage - as though he was still thinking of his confrontation with the doctor.

My mother was upstairs and I was laying the breakfast things for the Captain's return, when the front door creaked open and a man entered. He was a pale, twitching, sickly creature, with two fingers missing from his left hand. There was a cutlass hanging at his side, but he didn't look much of a fighting man. I still had my eyes open for seafarers, no matter how many legs they possessed, and I studied the stranger carefully. He didn't look like a sailor, but there was something about him that reminded me of the restless sea.

"What can I do for you, sir?" I asked politely.

"Bring rum," he said softly.

I turned to fetch a bottle, but he slid into a chair and gestured to me impatiently. "Come here first, sonny," he said. "Come nearer."

I took a step towards him.

"Is this breakfast you're serving for my mate, Bill?" he enquired slyly.

"I don't know your friend," I answered. "It's for a guest, and we call him the Captain."

"I see," he said, stroking his bony chin. "That's the kind of name my mate Bill would give himself. I wonder if it's him. He has a scar on his cheek, and a gentle way about him, especially when he's got some rum in his belly. Maybe your Captain has a cut on his cheek - the right cheek, perhaps? You see," he said with a smile, noting my reaction, "it must be him. Now, is he up in his room?"

"He's out on one of his walks, sir."

"Which way did he go, sonny?" he asked me gently.

When I told him, and answered other questions about which path the Captain was likely to return by, and how soon, the man chuckled. "Oh, he'll be pleased to see me, will my mate Bill."

I had no reason to agree with him, and I didn't like the expression on his face. But I decided it wasn't any of my business, so I returned to my chores.

I noticed the stranger didn't touch his rum. He kept

pacing around the bar-room, peering around the corner of the door, like a cat waiting for a mouse. When I stepped into the road to get something, he called me back urgently. But I didn't obey fast enough for his liking and a horrible change came over his ratlike features. "Get in," he snapped, adding an oath that made me shiver.

As soon as I was in the room, he settled back into his fawning, crafty manner, patting me on the shoulder with his filthy, ragged hands.

"I've taken quite a liking to you, really," he told me. "I have a boy, just like you. But you need discipline, sonny. If you'd sailed with Bill you wouldn't need telling twice what to do. That wasn't how Bill ran things. And here he is, bless him," he said suddenly, peering out through the window. "You and me will just step behind the door and give him a nice surprise."

He herded me into a gloomy corner behind the open door. I felt uneasy hiding there, and it only made me more nervous when I realized the stranger was frightened himself. He was gripping the hilt of his cutlass and the muscles in his face and neck twitched.

The Captain came in and marched straight over to his breakfast table.

"Bill," called the stranger, stepping into the light. He tried to sound bold, but I could hear the tremor in his voice. Then the Captain turned on his heel. I was shocked by the look on his face. It was as though he was staring at a ghost - or the devil.

"Come, Bill," hissed the stranger. "You must remember an old shipmate like me?"

"Black Dog," the Captain gasped.

"The one and only," the man replied, his confidence returning. "Black Dog's come to see his old shipmate, Billy. And it looks like we've both seen hard times since I lost these two talons." He held up his mutilated hand and grinned.

"So, you've tracked me down," the Captain grunted. "What is it you want?"

"You never did mince your words," laughed Black Dog. "Let's have a glass of rum, and sit down and talk things over like old shipmates."

When I came back with a jug, I found them seated at the Captain's breakfast table. Black Dog was sitting sideways on his chair, one eye fixed firmly on the Captain, the other on the door to the road.

"Now leave us," snapped Black Dog, waving me away.

From the other room I couldn't make out their whispers, but after a few minutes their voices grew louder and I could pick out a word or two, mostly the Captain's oaths.

"No, never," he cried suddenly. "If it comes to the rope, then you can go to the scaffold for all I care."

There was an explosion of swearing and furniture being thrown around, then the ring of steel on steel followed by a yelp of pain. I saw Black Dog dash into the road, pursued by the Captain. Both men had drawn their cutlasses, and blood was oozing from Black Dog's shoulder. The Captain lifted his sword arm to deliver a last tremendous stroke. He would

have sliced Black Dog from crown to chin, if the big *Admiral Benbow* sign hanging over our door hadn't been in the way of his blade. To this day, you can still see the notch he cut into the side of it.

The fight was over. Despite his wounds, Black Dog fled quickly away, while the Captain stared up at the inn sign, dazzled and disbelieving. I watched him sweep a hand over his eyes several times, then stagger into the house.

"Jim," he called. "Rum." His legs were wobbling, and he had to grip the wall to keep himself upright.

"Are you hurt?" I cried.

"Rum," he repeated. "Then I must leave. Rum," he screamed.

As I ran to the bar I heard a mighty crash behind me. The Captain was lying motionless, stretched out amid the broken glass and splinters of wood on the floor. By the time I reached his side, my mother had joined us, alerted by the commotion. We managed to lift the Captain's head, but his face was a bloodless white, his eyes were closed and his breathing came loud and hard.

"Oh Jim," my mother cried. "What a disgrace on the house! And your poor father at death's door himself."

Desperate to revive our guest, we struggled to pour some rum down his throat. But his jaws were locked together like a vice. Suddenly, Dr. Livesey stepped into the room, on his way to call on my father.

"Doctor," we cried. "Tell us, where is the poor man wounded?"

"Wounded?" scoffed Livesey, kneeling down next to the Captain's chest. "He's no more wounded than you or I. This man's had a stroke, just as I said he would. Mrs. Hawkins, why don't you run up to settle your husband, while I try to save this ruffian's worthless life. Jim, fetch a basin."

When I returned, the doctor had already rolled the Captain's sleeve, exposing a great sinewy arm covered with tattoos. "Here's Luck" said one of them; "A Fair Wind" and "Billy Bones" were others. Near his shoulder, there was a faded sketch of a gallows with a man hanging from its rope.

"Prophetic, I'd say," said the doctor, tapping this tattoo with one finger. "And now, master Billy Bones, let's have a pint out of you. You're not afraid of a little blood are you, Jim?"

"No, sir," I answered firmly.

"Then hold the basin steady," he ordered, expertly opening a vein with his scalpel.

We took a lot of blood before the Captain opened his eyes and looked mistily about him. He frowned when he recognized the doctor, but when he noticed me he seemed relieved. Then, suddenly, his forehead knotted and his eyes flashed: "Where's Black Dog?" he gasped.

"There's no dog here," replied the doctor coolly, "but you'll soon have the hounds of hell chasing after you if you're not careful. I've just dragged you from the grave. You've had a stroke, Mr. Bones…"

"That's not my name," the Captain interrupted.

"As if I care," responded Livesey dryly. "It's the name of a pirate I know, and I'll use it for the sake of convenience. If you keep drinking rum, I'll stake my precious wig it will kill you, and quickly. Be a man now, and curb your drinking. I'll help you to your bed, but only this once, mind."

We managed to drag the Captain upstairs and lie him out on the sheets. His head fell back across the pillow as though he was in a dead sleep.

"Remember what I said," added the doctor sternly. "Rum means death for you, Billy Bones."

He took me by the arm and led me from the room. Out in the hall, he stared at me intently: "He should lie quietly where he is for a week. One more stroke, and you'll have a dead man on your hands, Jim Hawkins."

At noon, I took a tray of cold drinks and medicine to the Captain's room. He was still resting on the bed, but had dragged himself up to a sitting position and looked both weak and excited.

"Jim," he cried. "You're the only one around here who's any good. I'm glad we've become friends. Haven't I always given you a silver coin at the end of each month? You can see I'm in trouble, deserted by everyone I trust. But I trust you, Jim. Fetch me a jug of rum..."

"But the doctor's orders," I protested.

"Swabs, that's all doctors are," he growled fiercely. "And that doctor knows nothing about sailors. I've been in places as hot as pitch, watched my friends dropping all around me with yellow fever, and felt the earth under my feet trembling with earthquakes and typhoons. What does Livesey know about that? I've lived on rum. It's been food and drink, man and wife to me. If I don't have rum, I'll die for sure, like an old wrecked ship on a desert shore. I'm already getting the horrors."

He lifted his shaking hands. "Can't keep them still," he panted. "I've just seen old Flint smiling at me from the corner, plain as the day. One glass won't hurt me, Jim, I'll give you gold for it."

I was worried that the noise he was making might disturb my father - who seemed weaker than ever that morning. And his offer of a bribe had roused my anger.

"Be quiet," I snapped. "I want none of your gold, except what you owe my father. I'll get you one glass, and no more."

When I returned, he drained the rum in one, greedy gulp.

"That's better," he hissed. "Now, how long did the doctor say I should stay in this bunk?"

"You must rest for a week," I replied.

"Thunder," he cursed. "They'll have the Black Spot on me before then. They're already circling like hungry sharks. They've lost what they had and want to steal mine. But I've saved what I earned, Jim, and mean to hang onto it. I'll leave them lost in a maze of reefs while I slip away."

He reared up on the bed, gripping my shoulder so tightly I almost shrieked in agony. But, despite all his brave talk, when he tried to swing his legs to the floor the effort was too much for him. He fell back, exhausted.

"Livesey's sucked all the blood out of me," he whimpered. He was silent for a moment, mustering his strength. "Did you see that man today, Jim?" he asked suddenly.

"Black Dog?"

"Aye. He's dangerous, he is, but nothing compared to the men who sent him. If I can't get away, they'll pass me the Black Spot and come for my chest. That's what they're after. You must get on a horse, Jim, and ride to the doctor. Tell him to order all hands on deck, the authorities that is. Bring them here and they'll catch Flint's crew, every one of them that's still alive. I was his first mate, Jim, the only one he trusted. He gave me the chest at Savannah, when he lay dying, as I do now. But don't raise the alarm until they get the Black Spot on me, or if you see Black Dog - or the seafaring man with only one leg. He's the worst of them all, Jim."

"But what is the Black Spot?" I asked him.

"Justice," he replied in a hushed voice. "Now keep your eyes open and I'll give you a share of everything. I give you my word."

He fell into a deep sleep, leaving me more confused than ever.

But I had other things to worry about than black spots and old Mr. Flint - whoever he was. That evening, my father died. As well as trying to cope with my own grief and my mother's distress, I had to organize the funeral and run the inn. I ignored the Captain, as he wandered around the house, helping himself to rum from the bar and locking himself away in his room. His drinking was worse than ever. The night before the funeral, he was singing his ugly sea shanties. Shocking as this was in a house of mourning, we didn't dare challenge him. The doctor had been called away to a far-flung corner of the parish, and we were alone with the tyrant.

Although he was walking about and taking meals again, the Captain seemed to grow weaker. He rarely left the inn, only putting his nose out of the door to sniff the sea, breathing heavily like a man climbing a mountain. He never mentioned the mysterious conversation we'd had in his room. Weak as he was, his temper was fierce. When he was drinking, he placed his cutlass on the table, as a warning to everyone to stay away. He seemed lost in his thoughts, mumbling to himself, singing old, tender songs he must have learned as a youth, before giving himself to the sea.

On the day after the funeral, I was gazing out towards the cove thinking of my poor father when I saw a figure on the road. It was a bitter, foggy afternoon and the air was quite murky, but I could see enough of the man to realize he was blind, possibly a beggar. He tapped at the path with a long, knotted stick, and had a green cloth shade fixed over his eyes and nose. Hunched over with age or infirmity, he wore a tattered old sea cloak with a hood that made him appear twisted and deformed. I had never seen a shabbier, more dreadful looking figure than this stooping blind man.

"Is there a kind lad here?" he cried in a high, thin voice, "who will help a poor man who lost his eyes in the service of his country and King George, God bless him? Where might I be?"

"At the *Admiral Benbow*, Black Hill Cove," I told him.

"I hear a young man's voice," he said warmly. "Will you give me your hand, laddie, and guide me in?"

Quickly, I stretched out my arm to help him. But his long fingers closed around my wrist like steel claws, and when I struggled he dragged me closer to his withered, eyeless face.

"Boy," he hissed. "Take me to the Captain."

"I can't," I cried. "I wouldn't dare."

"Take me in, or I'll snap your arm in two."

He tightened his grip until I squealed in pain.

"But, sir," I tried to tell him, "it's for your own safety. He has his cutlass ready and has already been fighting with another man."

"Walk!" he commanded. I had never heard a voice so cruel, cold and ugly. To listen to it was worse than the burning pain in my arm. I led him into the barroom, where the Captain was hunched over at his table.

"Take me right up to him," the blind man ordered, leaning all his weight on my aching arm. "When I'm close, I want you to shout, *"Here's a friend for you, Bill."* And don't fail me."

He squeezed my arm so tightly I thought I would faint with the pain. I was so terrified, I forgot all my fear of the Captain and cried out the words.

When the Captain flicked his eyes open, he looked like a man staring death in the face. He tried to stand, but there wasn't enough strength left in his body.

"Sit, Bill," ordered the blind man. "Don't move for

your sword. I might be blind but my ears can hear a finger twitch. This is business. Boy," he barked, "give me his left hand."

I slowly pulled the Captain's huge, open paw across the table, and the blind man slipped something between the fingers.

"It's done," he hissed. The next second he had released me. As nimble as a goat, he backed out of the room and went tap-tap-tapping into the fog that swirled around the inn.

The Black Spot

It took several seconds before the Captain recovered his senses. Finally, I watched him snatch his hand back and stare into his palm.

"Ten o'clock," he cried. "Only six hours, but we'll beat them yet."

He staggered to his feet, but the sudden effort was too much for his heart. I watched as he lifted a shaking hand to his throat, teetered like a tree about to fall, then smashed face-first into the floorboards.

I was at his side in a second and calling to my mother. But there was no use hurrying. The Captain was dead. Even though I had lived in fear of the man, only pitying him as he steadily drank himself to death, the tears were streaming from my eyes. This was the second death in our house and the loss of my father was still fresh in my heart.

When my mother arrived, I described what I'd seen, and repeated the conversation I'd had with the Captain after his first stroke.

"You should have told me before, Jim," my mother cried. "Don't you see the danger we're in?"

She was right, of course, but I couldn't help feeling that we were entitled to some of the Captain's money - if he had some locked away in his trunk. Dr. Livesey would help us, but if I rode off to fetch him that would leave my mother alone and unprotected. The more I thought about our situation, the more terrified I became. Every sound made me jump, and the sight of the Captain's dead body reminded me of the shuffling blind man, groping his way through the fog. I decided our best chance for safety was for us both to walk over to the hamlet and ask for help.

We left without delay, stepping into the ice-cold fog around the inn. The hamlet lay on the far side of the next cove, and we hurried along the path towards it, listening out for any strange sound in the night air. I was as jumpy as a cat, but the only noise was the ripple of the surf and a frog croaking in the woods.

My heart soared when I saw the candles flickering in the houses ahead of us. Here were our friends and protectors, I thought to myself. But I was quite wrong. Although we went to every house, not a soul would agree to join us at the inn. As soon as I mentioned the name *Flint*, some of the men recoiled in horror. Other villagers said they'd seen strangers on the cliff road, and a ship with no markings at anchor in Kitt's Hole, a quiet bay along the coast. They wanted nothing to do with Flint and his crew. Although they offered to ride to Dr. Livesey's house to raise the alarm, they refused to help defend the inn.

My mother tried to stem their cowardice by making a bold and heartfelt speech. "I will not," she declared, "lose money that belongs to my poor, fatherless boy. If none of you men are brave enough, then Jim and I will go alone. We'll have that chest open if we die for it, won't we, Jim?"

I nodded, of course. The villagers tried to persuade us to stay, then gave me a loaded pistol and promised to have horses saddled and waiting in case of emergency. They also sent a lad to find the doctor.

My heart was beating wildly when we left the candlelit glow of the hamlet and stepped into the night. There was a full moon beaming through the fog, and anyone could have seen us walking along the path towards the inn. But we slipped around the cove, silent and swift, and didn't see or hear anything suspicious. Perhaps we were in no danger at all, but still I let out a sigh of relief when the heavy, oak door of the *Admiral Benbow* was bolted firmly behind us.

We stood panting for breath for a few seconds, alone in the dark house with the dead Captain. When we'd recovered our nerves, my mother fetched a candle. Holding each other's hand, we stepped closer to his body. His eyes were open and glaring, and one arm was stretched out in a spasm of pain.

"Pull the blinds down, Jim," my mother whispered. "They might be watching."

When I came back, she shook her head in dismay: "We have to get the key off the corpse," she said, with a shudder.

I knelt down by the Captain at once, sparing my mother the gruesome task of searching his body. On the floor by his outstretched hand I noticed a torn piece of paper blackened on one side - the black spot.

When I examined it, I saw a short message written on the other side:

You have until ten tonight.

"They're coming at ten," I whispered to my mother. As I finished speaking, our old grandfather clock began striking. The noise was a terrible shock, but it was a piece of good luck.

"It's only six," my mother whispered. "Get the key, Jim."

Rummaging in his pockets, I pulled out an assortment of nautical junk: a thimble and thread, some coins, chewing tobacco, a sailor's knife, pocket compass and tinder box.

"Try around his neck," she whispered.

I had to grit my teeth to do it, but I ripped open his shirt and padded my fingers around the cold skin at his neck. There was a piece of greasy string tied there. I cut it free and there was the key.

We were upstairs in seconds, dragging the old sea chest into the middle of his room. It had the initial *B* branded into the wooden lid, and the corners were chipped and worn with long, rough usage.

"Give me the key," ordered my mother. Although the lock was stiff, she had the chest open in a flash.

There was a pungent smell of tar and tobacco. But when I looked down, all I could see was a suit of clothes, of the finest quality, carefully brushed and folded.

"Never been worn," muttered my mother, lifting them out gently. Under the suit, we saw the medley of possessions that made up the Captain's life: a ship's quadrant, a small tin cup, sticks of tobacco, four pistols with intricate decoration, a bar of silver, a Spanish watch and other trinkets, two compasses and a clutch of strange, exotic shells lifted from some tropical beach. What would a man like the Captain want with these shells, I wondered, in his wandering, guilty and hunted life?

We searched deeper into the chest, looking for a few gold coins that would settle his bill at the inn. Under the shells and other relics, we found an old cloak, crusted white with sea salt from a thousand ocean voyages. But hidden beneath this cloak were the last two items in the chest: a bundle of papers wrapped in oilskin and a canvas bag that bulged with coins.

"I'll show these ruffians that I'm an honest woman," my mother declared proudly. "I'll take what's owed to me and not a penny more."

We began sorting through the coins, which was no easy matter. The Captain had collected a great assortment of currencies, from every port and country - doubloons, pieces of eight, French gold and English guineas. While we were picking out the guineas, I suddenly grabbed my mother by the arm.

"What is it, Jim?" she whispered.

I had heard a sound that made me shiver - the tap of the blind man's stick on the frozen path. It came closer and closer, while we sat holding our breath.

There was a knock at the outside door and we heard the handle creak. The bolt rattled, then there was silence. Finally, after an agonizing wait, I heard the sound of his tapping again, fading away as he vanished into the fog.

"Take it all, mother," I whispered. "We can't wait another minute."

"I'm an honest woman," she replied firmly. "There's enough time left to sort out these coins. It isn't even seven yet."

She went on talking while I thought about the bolted door downstairs. Perhaps it would make the pirates suspicious? My mother was still muttering when we heard a low whistle coming from the hill above the inn.

"This will do," she cried, jumping to her feet with a handful of coins.

"I'll take this," I told her, snatching the oilskin packet. "To make up the difference."

In an instant, we were groping our way downstairs, leaving the candle by the pillaged chest. I unbolted the door and we darted into the night. Just in time. The fog around the house was lifting, and most of the building was in bright moonlight. Only the door and the low ground towards the cove was still shrouded. I heard footsteps and saw a lantern dancing towards us along the path through the fog.

"Take the money and run, Jim," my mother sobbed.

We were trapped like rats. I began cursing our cowardly friends in the hamlet, and my mother's honesty and greed for keeping us at the inn so long.

But suddenly, the fog swirled to one side and I saw where we were. There was still a chance. To my right I spotted the little bridge over the stream. I helped my mother down the bank and managed to drag her under the bridge arch. She had passed out in shock or fright, and I couldn't carry her any further. We were partially hidden, sheltered by the bank of the stream, but we were still only yards from the inn. If the fog cleared we would be spotted instantly.

My curiosity must have been stronger than my fear, because I found myself peeping over the bank. Seven or eight men burst out of the fog. The man with the lantern ran in front, and bringing up the rear was a group of three, with their hands joined together like a trio of children at play. The blind man was in the middle, using his two companions to guide the way.

"Kick down the door," he screeched.

"Aye, aye, sir," called two of the men, and rushed at the inn. When they found the door was open they paused, but the blind man ordered them inside, screaming in a frenzy of excitement and rage.

"Get in with you," he cried.

He waited in the road, while I heard the sound of stamping feet and crashing doors inside the inn.

"Bill's dead," came a shout.

"Never mind that," yelled the blind man. "Search him. Find the chest."

The stairs creaked and groaned with the weight of the raiders, then a window in the Captain's room flew open so violently one of its glass panes shattered. A man stuck his head out into the moonlight and called down: "Pew, someone's beaten us to it. They've turned Billy's chest inside out."

"Is it still there?" demanded Pew.

"The money is."

"Curse the money," Pew screamed. "Are Flint's papers there?"

"None," came the answer.

I saw the blind man's lips curl back over his teeth in fury. "It's the people of the inn," he howled. "I wish I'd blinded that boy. But they were here no time ago. They've slipped out. Scatter lads. Seek them out."

The house exploded with noise as the raiders went from room to room, searching for us. At last, satisfied the house was empty, they hurried down to the road and began kicking through the grass and bushes. I was sure we would be discovered. But suddenly I heard the whistle from the hill again, sounding twice.

"That's Dirk," cried a man. "We'll have to clear off, mates."

"You're not running yet," hissed Pew. "Dirk's a coward. Ignore him. That woman and boy must be round here. Get looking for them, you dogs. You'd see some horrors if I only had my eyes."

Some men went back to the search, but a knot of them waited in the road, staring nervously into the fog.

"You're so close to millions," Pew spat at them, "but you waste time fretting. Find the boy. Why should I be a beggar for the rest of my life, pleading for rum, when I could be rolling in a coach like a lord? Catch them."

"We've got Bill's coins, Pew," one of the men reasoned. "That's enough. Let's run."

Pew's rage welled up inside him, until he wheeled about with his staff, striking his own men. They cursed and tried to grab his stick. While they squabbled, we were safe, but suddenly I heard the sound of horses galloping along the cliff path. There was a pistol shot from the cove, a last signal for the raiders. They turned and ran in all directions, dashing over the hill, down to the sea and away into the fog. Only Pew was left behind.

"Morgan," he cried desperately, "Black Dog, Dirk, don't leave me. You won't leave old Pew, mates."

Four riders broke out of the fog at the top of the hill, charging along the road. Pew screamed in terror at the sound of hooves hitting the earth, and ran straight into a ditch. He tumbled over, pulled himself up and tottered towards the hill, but in his panic he

turned again, tripping into the path of the first horse.

The rider tried to rein his mount, but it was too late. With an awful scream, I saw Pew trampled and crushed as the stallion rode over his body. He rolled to the side of the road, then slumped forwards and was still. It was the end of the blind man.

Captain's Papers

I was up on my feet in a second, hailing the riders. At the rear of the pack I recognized the lad from the village. He had been riding to the doctor's when he'd chanced on a customs patrol, led by Captain Dance, who had the sense to break off his mission and hurry to the inn. This chance patrol was the only thing that had saved us from a horrible death.

A quick glance at Pew was enough to establish he was stone dead. As for my mother, once she'd sipped some cool water she was her old self, complaining again about the unsettled bill. But when we stepped inside the *Admiral Benbow*, I saw at once we were ruined.

"Incredible," cried Captain Dance. "What were they searching for that made them smash every object?"

"I believe, sir," I replied, "that I have the answer in my breast-pocket. I must find a safe place for it."

"Of course," he said with a smile. "Let me keep it."

"I was thinking of showing it to Dr. Livesey," I stammered.

"Quite right," he said cheerfully. "He's a gentleman and a magistrate, after all. He's with Squire Trelawney tonight, I believe, and I need to see them to make my report. Master Pew is dead and, though I couldn't care less about the wretch, I must make an official statement, so nobody can accuse us of wrongdoing. We'll ride to the squire's house together."

"Dogger," he called to one of his men, "this boy

rides with you."

After quickly explaining to my mother where I was going, I jumped up into the saddle behind Dogger. The next instant we were bouncing along the coast road at a fast trot, on our way to the squire's hall.

We soon entered a long, moonlit avenue that led up to the hall. Dance and I dismounted and climbed the steps at the front of the house. We were met by a butler, who led us down a hallway covered in deep rugs and into a great library. On every wall there were shelves and statues, and the squire and doctor were seated at a blazing fire, puffing away at their pipes.

I was only a country boy, and had never been so close to the squire before. He was a tall, stocky man, and his face was ruddy and lined from years of travel. His eyebrows were huge and black, and made him look fierce, like a hawk.

"Come in," he ordered.

"Evening Dance," added the doctor calmly. "Hello, Jim. What good wind brings you here?"

The Captain gave a full account of the adventure at the inn, while both gentlemen sat forward in their chairs, so amazed by the story they forgot their pipes altogether. When they heard how my mother had dared to return to the inn, Livesey slapped his thigh. The squire cried "Bravo" and then jumped out of his chair and began pacing the room. Livesey removed his white wig so he could hear the Captain's report more clearly.

"You are a noble fellow," the squire announced, when Dance had finished. "As for riding down that atrocious rascal Pew, I regard it as a decent act, like stamping on a cockroach. This boy Hawkins is obviously a stout, hearty lad. Ring that bell, boy, and we'll get Mr. Dance some ale."

"So, Jim," said the doctor, "do you have what they were after?"

I handed him the oilskin packet and, although I could see he was aching to tear it open, he hesitated, placing it carefully inside his frock coat. "Squire," he said, "when Dance has finished his ale he must be off on the King's business, but with your permission I would like Jim Hawkins to stay. He can sleep at my house tonight and, in the meantime, perhaps we can offer him a piece of pie?"

"He's earned it," chortled the squire.

A few minutes later, I was enjoying a large wedge of pigeon pie. I was just finishing the last mouthful when the squire finally dismissed Captain Dance from the room.

"Well, squire," said the doctor. "You have heard of this man Flint, I suppose?"

"Heard of him?" roared the squire. "He was the most bloodthirsty buccaneer ever. Compared to him, Blackbeard was like an innocent child. The Spaniards were so terrified of him, I confess there were times I was proud he was an Englishman. And I've seen his pirate ship with my own eyes, sir, off the island of Trinidad. The yellow-bellied coward that was my captain turned back to port when he saw Flint on the horizon."

"Even I," said the doctor modestly, "have heard of Flint. But the question is, did he have any money?"

"Money?" the squire bellowed. "What else were these rascals risking their carcasses for but money?"

"We shall soon find out," replied the doctor. "But, you shout and bluster so much, dear squire, I can hardly get a word in. Tell me, was Flint rich?"

"If we have a clue to his treasure," said the squire, "I will take you and Jim Hawkins to Bristol, fit out a ship. We'll find Flint's gold, if it takes us a year of searching."

"Very well," said the doctor. "In that case, gather round. With Jim's permission, we'll open this packet."

He laid the oilskin bundle on the table before him. It was sewn together, so the doctor had to rummage through his instruments to find some surgical scissors to cut it open. A small book and a roll of parchment dropped onto the table.

"Let's try the book first," suggested the doctor.

On the first page there were doodles and scraps of writing, and I recognized some of the same phrases and designs we'd discovered on Billy Bones' corpse. I shuddered when I saw one line: "Off Palm Key he got it." I couldn't help wondering who it was that *got it*, and what *it* was he got.

"Not much use," the doctor snapped, turning over the page.

As he flicked through the book, I saw a series of neat entries, each with a date, several crosses, and a sum of money. There were some coordinates and place names beside the entries. For example, on June 12, 1745, someone had received 70 pounds, *off Caracas*.

"I'm afraid I'm baffled," declared the doctor, shaking his head.

"But it's clear as day," beamed the squire. "This is the black-hearted rogue's account book. The crosses represent the towns or ships his ship plundered, and the sums of money are his share of the loot. God help the poor souls he robbed off Caracas, thrown to the sharks no doubt. And look at the last entries! They come almost 20 years after the first."

"Of course," cried the doctor. "Beware the perils of travel, Jim. Billy Bones was prowling the oceans, amassing a fortune. You can see the amounts increase with time, to match his rise in rank."

"Enough mathematics," cried Squire Trelawney impatiently. "Let's have a look at the other item."

The doctor opened the roll of paper carefully, and a small map fell onto the table. It was a sketch of an island, showing latitude and longitude, the names of hills, bays and rivers, and every other detail needed to bring a ship into safe anchorage. The island was nine miles long and five wide, shaped like a fat little dragon standing on its heels. There were two bays for mooring a ship, and a hill in the middle of the island called *The Spyglass*. Scratched into the map in blood-red ink were three crosses. Next to one of them, Billy Bones had written: *bulk of treasure here*. The doctor flipped the map over, to reveal some writing in the same red ink.

Tall tree. Spy glass, North to North East.
Skeleton Island East South East.
Go ten feet.
Bar silver in the north.
Ten fathoms south of black crag.
Arms are easily found, in the sand hill.
North of north inlet.
J.F.

"Livesey!" roared the squire, throwing his hands up in delight. "You will abandon your wretched patients at once. I go to Bristol tomorrow, to find a vessel. In three weeks - no, in ten days - we'll have the best ship and the finest crew in England. Hawkins shall join us as cabin boy. You'll make a splendid sailor, Jim Hawkins. You, Livesey, will be ship's doctor, and I will take the position of admiral. We'll take my best three servants with us. With a good wind we'll be at the island in no time. We'll have money to play with, to roll in like hogs, for the rest of our days.

"Squire Trelawney," interrupted the doctor, getting to his feet. "I will join you, and will work my heart out for this mission, as will Jim, I'm sure. But there is one man," he said seriously, "who makes me worry."

"Name the dog, sir," ordered the squire. "Who is it?"

"You," snapped the doctor. "You're a chatterbox, Trelawney. We're not the only ones who know about this map. Those pirates who attacked the inn are determined to get Flint's riches. They'd cut our throats for this map. We must be on our guard until we get to sea. So, remember: don't breathe a word of this voyage to a living soul."

"Livesey," the squire answered firmly, "you may count on me. I'll be as silent as the grave."

The Sea Cook

It was several weeks before we were ready to set off on our treasure hunt. I lived at the hall, with old Redruth, the gamekeeper, as my guardian. The doctor had gone to London to find a physician willing to take charge of his practice, while the squire stayed in Bristol making preparations for the voyage. Most of the time I was left alone with my thoughts, dreaming of the sea, exotic islands and adventures. The map of Treasure Island was fixed in my mind. I brooded over it for hours, sitting by a glowing fire in the housekeeper's room, exploring every acre of its surface in my imagination. From the top of the Spyglass, I studied the ocean and the wild, rocky shores. Sometimes, we were battling savages and cannibals. In other dreams, we hunted dangerous beasts, or were stalked through thick forests. But, in all these daydreams, nothing ever happened that was as strange as our real adventure.

At last, we received a letter, addressed to Livesey, Redruth and myself. I tore it open and, as Redruth had been a poor student at school, read it aloud.

Old Anchor Inn, Bristol, March 1st

Dear Friends,

The ship is ready. She lies at anchor, hungry for the sea. You've never seen a sweeter schooner, 200 tonnes, and her name - the Hispaniola.

An old friend, Blandly, found her for me. He's been slaving away on my behalf ever since I arrived in Bristol, as have so many others, as soon as they heard about our voyage to find the treasure.

"The squire has been talking," I gasped. "Dr. Livesey won't be happy about this."

"So?" growled the gamekeeper, loyally. "The squire can say what he wants. Get on with it."

Blandly bought the ship on my behalf. There are some rascals who seem to hold a grudge against my friend. They say he's owned the Hispaniola for years and sold it to me for an exorbitant amount. But of course they are fools. I can tell a jewel of a ship when I see one.

We had some trouble finding a suitable crew. I wanted 20 brave men, but it was hard to find more than half a dozen hands, until I had a stroke of luck.

I was standing on the dock when I met an old sailor who keeps a public house with his Caribbean wife, and knows all the seafaring men along the coast. Life on dry land was ruining his health, he told me, and he was desperate to find a berth as a cook on some long ocean voyage. He had hobbled down to the docks that morning, just to get a good sniff of the sea air.

I was terribly charmed by his story, as would you have been, Livesey. Long John Silver is his name. He served under the noble Captain Hawke, and lost his leg in a naval battle for our country. He has no pension, Livesey, although he has some savings and a bank account which has never been overdrawn. I offered him a job immediately.

Well, sir, I thought I'd found a cook, but it turned out I'd discovered a whole crew. Silver introduced me to some of the toughest old salts you could imagine - not pretty to look at, but we have a crew strong enough to fight a frigate. Long John even helped to weed out a few weak sailors from the men I'd already engaged. They lacked the stamina and experience we need for our voyage.

I am fit as a fiddle, eating like a bull, sleeping like a log, but I'm still longing to get under way and taste saltwater spray on my lips. Forget the treasure! It's the glory of the ocean that makes my heart race. Get here as quickly as you can. Don't waste one hour.

Young Hawkins, go at once to your mother and say your farewell, then come full speed to Bristol.

Yours, John Trelawney.

p.s. Blandly has promised to send a navy ship to search for us if we haven't returned by the end of August. He has also found me a captain - a gifted navigator and seaman, but rather stern, I'm afraid. Long John Silver proposed a very competent man to serve as first mate.

p.p.s. Jim Hawkins may spend one night with his mother.

The squire's letter was the answer to all my hopes and daydreams: we were finally going to sea. I was beside myself with excitement - unlike old Tom Redruth, who could only complain about his miserable luck. He didn't want to leave the village, let alone the country. Any of the junior gamekeepers would have jumped at the chance to go off hunting treasure, but this wasn't the squire's pleasure - and the squire's pleasure was law among his servants. Nobody but old Redruth would have dared to grumble about his orders.

In the morning, we set out for the *Admiral Benbow*. I was relieved to find my mother in good health, and the inn was looking better than ever. Squire Trelawney had paid for all the damages and bought us new furniture - even the sign had been repainted. The squire had also hired a young boy to help my mother run the inn. The sight of him reminded me of everything I was leaving behind me: the old inn, my former life and my dear mother. That night, I had my first attack of tears since the sight of the Captain's body, stretched out on the bar-room floor.

The following afternoon, I said good-bye to my mother and the cove where I had always lived, and Redruth and I started along the cliff path. A mail coach picked us up outside the *Royal George* inn. Despite all the shaking and the cold night air, I soon fell into a deep sleep. I was only awakened by a sharp tap in the ribs. I opened my eyes to see a large building in a city street, in the bright sunlight of a new day.

"Where are we?" I asked.

"Bristol, of course," replied Tom. "Down you come."

The squire was staying at an inn by the docks. As we walked over there I saw the port's long quays and a great fleet of ships at anchor. They were of all sizes and nations. The sailors in one ship were singing on the decks; in another, they were high in the rigging, hanging to threads that seemed no thicker than a spider's web. The smell of tar and sea salt was new to me, even though I'd lived by the coast all my life. At every step I saw something that amazed me. Some of the ships had great figureheads, worn and faded from years of roaming the world's oceans. Old sailors swaggered past me in a clumsy, rolling sea walk. They had rings in their ears, long pigtails and curled beards. A procession of kings and archbishops couldn't have been more fascinating.

While I was still dazzled by these sights and sounds, we met Squire Trelawney outside his inn. He was in a sea officer's uniform of thick blue cloth, and he had a broad smile on his face.

"Here you are," he cried. "And the doctor arrived last night, so the ship's company is complete."

"When do we sail, sir?" I shouted in my excitement.

"Tomorrow, Jim Hawkins," he chuckled.

After treating me to a huge breakfast at the inn, the squire sent me off with a note for his new friend, John Silver.

"You will find his tavern, *The Spyglass*," he told me, "by keeping a lookout for a telescope hanging over its door."

I set off at once, overjoyed at the prospect of seeing more ships and sailors. It was mid-morning, the busiest time along the waterfront. The quay was crowded with people, carts and stores, but I soon found the tavern, a large room hazy with tobacco smoke. But it wasn't a gloomy place. The curtains were clean and the floorboards were freshly sanded. On either side of the house there was an open door leading out to the street, so the interior was full of light. As for the customers, they were a rough crowd and I hung at the doorway almost afraid to enter.

While I waited, I saw a man step out of a side room. I was sure he must be Long John. His left leg was cut off close to the hip and he had a crutch jammed under his shoulder, which he used with wonderful dexterity. He hopped about on it like a bird, nimbly sweeping between the tables.

The man was tall and strong, with a huge, pale face that looked both friendly and intelligent. He seemed to be in the best of moods, whistling as he made his way to the bar, with a joke or amiable slap on the shoulder for his customers.

From the first mention of Long John Silver in the squire's letter, I had feared he might be the same rogue the Captain had paid me to watch for. But one glance at this man convinced me I was mistaken. I had seen the Captain, Black Dog and Pew, and I thought I knew what a pirate looked like. They were a savage breed compared to this well-scrubbed, smiling landlord.

Plucking up my courage, I stepped into the room and approached the one-legged man at the bar. "Mr. Silver, sir?" I asked, holding out the note.

"Yes, my lad," he replied smoothly, "that's my name. And who might you be?" And then, as he saw the squire's letter, he seemed to start with surprise. "Oh, I see," he said loudly. "You're the new cabin boy, Hawkins. Well I'm pleased to meet you."

He shook my hand, enclosing it in his large, firm grasp. I noticed a flicker at the corner of my eye and

turned to see a man rushing for the door to the street. He was gone in a flash, but I recognized him instantly: Black Dog.

"Stop him!" I cried. "Stop that man!"

"And he hasn't paid his bill," roared Silver. "Ben, run and catch him."

A man nodded and ran off in pursuit.

"Even if he were an admiral," cried Silver, "he can pay his bill like an honest sailor. Who did you say he was, lad?"

"Black Dog, sir," I answered. "Didn't the squire tell you about the buccaneers who ransacked my mother's inn? He was with them."

"No," gasped Silver. "A real pirate? And in my tavern. Come over here, Morgan, I saw you drinking with him."

An old, grey-haired sailor with a face tanned brown

as mahogany glanced up. He stepped forward sheepishly, chewing at a stub of tobacco.

"Now, Morgan," said Long John severely, "you've never clapped eyes on this Black Dog before, have you?"

"No, sir," coughed Morgan and shook his sun-scorched head.

"That's lucky for you, Tom Morgan," said Silver fiercely. "If you'd been mixed up with the likes of him I'd have banned you from my tavern. Now get back to your table and don't go talking to any pirates again."

As the old sailor shuffled back to his seat, Silver explained to me in a confidential whisper: "He's an honest man, but a fool, lad." I was flattered by this show of trust.

"I don't recognize the name Black Dog?" Silver continued. "But now I think of it, yes, I've seen the swab before. He used to come in with a blind beggar."

"His name was Pew," I shouted.

"Was it?" Silver gasped. "He looked a real shark. If we catch Black Dog we'll have some news for the squire, and there aren't many sailors who can outrun my friend Ben."

While he talked, he hopped around the tavern, slapping the tables with his enormous hands and puffing with rage. Any doubts I'd had about his trustworthiness were quickly dispelled. By the time the hunter returned and admitted he'd lost the quarry in a thick crowd, I thought Silver the most respectable man in the port.

"Look here, lad," Silver began apologetically. "This business is a stain on my character. What's the squire to think of me? You must put in a good word for me, Jim. After all, what could I do, with this old stump of oak for a leg? In the old days I would have caught him in a flash."

Suddenly his face turned bright red. "The bill," he burst out. "Shiver my timbers. I've lost three tumblers of rum to that scoundrel." Falling across a bench, Silver howled with laughter until the tears were streaming over his cheeks. "What an old sea lion pup I am," he cried. "We should get on well lad, for I'm no wiser than a cabin boy. But let's weigh anchor and be off to see the squire. It's my duty to report this business, even though neither of us will come out of it with any credit. At least we had a chuckle over my lost rum."

Strolling along the quay, Silver proved to be an entertaining and knowledgeable companion. He seemed to know every bit of gossip about the moored ships, which distant country they'd sailed from and where their next voyage would take them. His conversation was peppered with lively stories, and he even taught me some nautical terms. I began to see he was one of the best possible shipmates.

When we reached the inn, we found the squire and Dr. Livesey enjoying a tankard of ale before setting off to inspect the ship. Long John quickly told them every detail of the story, occasionally asking me to confirm the facts.

"A shame he escaped," cried the squire. "But it can't be helped."

Silver nodded, then explained that he must be

getting back to his inn.

"All hands on deck by four this afternoon, Silver," said the squire.

"Aye, aye, sir," answered the cook with a smile, then pushed his way into the dockside crowds.

"Well, Trelawney," said the doctor. "I don't know about your other discoveries here in Bristol, but I like John Silver."

"Solid as a rock," declared the squire.

"Indeed," replied the doctor. "And now, squire, may young Hawkins come on board with us?"

"But of course," laughed the squire. "It's about time Jim saw the ship."

Captain Smollett

The *Hispaniola* was anchored some way from the dockside and we had to row out to her, gliding around the sterns of the other packed ships, floating under their wave-worn figureheads. We pulled alongside a low schooner and were saluted by the mate, Mr. Arrow, as we climbed aboard. He was a bronzed "old salt" and it was clear that he and the squire were already firm friends. But Trelawney's relations with the ship's captain, Mr. Smollett, were a good deal more frosty. He was a sharp-faced man who looked angry with everything on board, and wanted to tell us why. No sooner had we sat down in the main cabin than a sailor entered, asking if the captain might speak with us.

"Show him in," the squire replied coolly. "I am always at the captain's attention."

Smollett ducked under the low doorway to the cabin and asked his messenger to leave.

"Well, captain," the squire began, "I hope everything is shipshape and seaworthy?"

"I believe it's best to speak plainly," replied Smollett, "even at the risk of offending you. I don't like this cruise of yours, I don't like the crew and I don't like my mate. That's it, short and sweet."

"Perhaps, sir," snapped the squire, "you don't like my ship?"

"I've yet to see how she performs at sea," Smollett answered. "But she looks a fine ship."

"What about your employer, sir?" asked the squire. "Do you care for him?"

But this was too much for Dr. Livesey. "Let's all calm down, squire," he said, trying to soothe him. "Questions like that will only lead to bad feeling between us and the captain. I think he has said too much or too little, and I want an explanation of his speech. Please, Captain Smollett, tell us why you don't like this voyage?"

"I was engaged to be captain under what sailors call *sealed orders*: that means I must pilot the ship to an unknown destination. So far, so good. But now I find that every man aboard knows more about our voyage than I do. I don't call that fair, do you?"

"No," said Livesey firmly. "I do not."

"Next," said the captain, crossing his arms, "I learn from my own crew that this is a treasure hunt. Now, hunting treasure is dangerous work and I don't like anything about it, least of all when the whole thing is supposed to be a secret, but everyone on the ship knows about it - including the parrot - except for the captain, which is me."

"You mean Silver's parrot?" gasped the squire.

"It's a figure of speech, sir," replied the captain patiently. "I'm saying the secret's out, and I don't think you gentlemen know what you're getting yourselves into. My guess is you'll be lucky to escape with your lives."

"That's clear enough," Livesey answered. "But we're not quite so ignorant as you imagine. We've accepted the risks involved. Next, you say you don't like the crew. Why not?"

"I should have been given the job of choosing my own men," Smollett responded.

"Perhaps you should," agreed the doctor. "But the squire didn't mean to insult you when he hired these men. What about the mate?"

"He's a good seaman," the captain conceded, "but he's too chummy with the crew. A mate should keep himself to himself, and not go drinking with the men."

"Are you saying he's a drunkard?" the squire cried.

"I'm only saying he's too familiar with the crew, sir," the captain answered.

"Let's get to the heart of this," the doctor interrupted. "What do you want, captain?"

"Are you determined to go on this cruise?" Smollett replied.

"Set like iron," answered the squire.

"Then listen to what I have to say. The crew are storing the weapons and gunpowder in the front hold. You have a good strong room under this cabin; put them there instead. Move your own men to berths nearby and keep them away from the front of the ship. And one more thing. There's been too much blabbing already."

"Far too much," agreed the doctor.

"I've heard that you have a map of the island. The treasure is marked by crosses and the coordinates are as follows…"

He named the position of the island precisely.

"But I didn't tell a soul about the island's location," the squire spluttered.

"Nevertheless, the sailors know it," said the captain.

"It must have been Livesey or Hawkins," the squire protested.

"It doesn't matter who's been talking," replied the doctor, ignoring the squire's denials. "But the cat's out of the bag."

"I don't know who has the map," added the captain. "And I don't want to know."

"I understand," the doctor told him. "We'll keep that secret, at least. If I'm not mistaken, you want us to make a fort of the rear of the ship, keeping all the arms and our most trusted men there. Do you fear a mutiny, captain?"

"You must not put words in my mouth, sir. If I was sure of mutiny, I wouldn't put out to sea. Mr. Arrow is honest, I believe, as are some of the crew. But I have a bad feeling about this voyage and simply want to take every precaution. Then we'll be safe."

"Is that everything, captain?" the doctor asked. "When you first came in here I would have bet my wig you were about to resign."

"So I was, sir," Smollett answered. "I didn't think the squire would listen to my complaint."

"If Livesey hadn't been here," continued the squire, "you'd have been on shore by now, looking for a job. As it is, I have listened and will do as you ask - but I think the worse of you."

"As you please, sir," answered Smollett. "You'll see what kind of man I am before too long."

With that he saluted, turned and left us.

"Squire," said the doctor after a few moments of silence, "contrary to my suspicions, I believe you've managed to find two honest men to aid us: Silver's one of them; the other just left the room."

"Our captain," snapped the squire, "is unmanly, unsailorly, and downright un-English."

"We'll see about that," replied the doctor, thoughtfully.

When we came on deck, the men were already making the changes Smollett had requested. I was happy to be getting one of the comfy berths in the rear of the ship, away from the damp confines of the forecastle. The doctor, the squire and I, as well as Redruth and the other two servants, Hunter and Joyce, all had proper beds in the stern. Captain Smollett and Arrow strung their hammocks in the hut that covered the entrance to the cabin quarters.

We were still hard at work, storing the rifles and powder below the cabin, when the last of the crew came aboard. Silver was among them. He clambered up the side of the ship with the agility of a monkey.

"What's all this, mates?" he cried when he saw the arms being moved to the stern.

"We're moving the powder," a sailor called out.

"But we'll miss the tide if we waste any time," argued Silver.

"Those are my orders," snapped the captain. "Get below and make the men some supper."

"Aye, sir," answered the cook, raising a finger to the brim of his hat in a salute.

"Easy with that powder," cried the captain, turning back to the men working on the deck. He spotted me examining the brass cannon we carried, mounted close to the main mast.

"Ship's boy," he roared at me, "go and help the cook with his work."

As I hurried below I heard him tell the doctor: "I'll have no idlers on my ship."

After that I shared the squire's opinion of my captain: I hated him.

All night long the sailors were busy preparing the ship for sea. Boatloads of the squire's friends arrived to wish him a safe and prosperous voyage. I was busier serving them drinks and snacks than I had ever been at the *Admiral Benbow*. Towards dawn, the mate sounded his pipe and the crew swarmed into the rigging. Even though I was almost asleep on my feet after so many hours of hard work, I couldn't leave the deck to go to my bunk. Everything about the ship was so new and interesting: the quick commands, shrill whistles and men hanging in the sails, the phantom shadows in the glimmer of the deck lanterns.

"Go on, Barbecue," shouted a sailor high in the masts, "give us a song."

"One of the old ones," cried another.

"Aye mates," Long John called out, answering to this nickname. He lifted his great head skywards: "Fifteen men on the dead man's chest," he roared. The whole crew picked up the words: "Yo - ho - ho, and a bottle of rum!"

They worked as they sang, and for a second I thought I could hear Billy Bones' rasping voice hidden among that choir of sailors. Suddenly, there was a screech of metal and I turned and saw the anchor rising from the waves, dripping as a sailor lashed it to the stern. Soon the sails were unfurled and I watched them fill with air. The land and the fleet of ships began flying by on either side. Before I could lay my head down on a pillow, *Hispaniola* had begun her voyage to Treasure Island.

After only a few days at sea, the captain's doubts seemed to have been blown away on the clean, ocean air. The *Hispaniola* proved to be a fine, sturdy ship, and her crew experienced seamen. But not all his fears were unfounded. It was obvious that Mr. Arrow hadn't won the respect of the men: they paid little attention to his orders. But that wasn't the worst of it. He began to appear on deck with dull eyes and red cheeks, the classic symptoms of a drunkard. Time after time, the captain sent him below in disgrace, but he was always stumbling about the ship injuring himself, or curled up in his bunk too drunk to stand.

We never discovered where he stashed his bottles. It was a complete mystery. The only place that had a ready supply of alcohol was the cook's cupboard and Silver guarded the key religiously. When we challenged the mate, he only laughed or denied that he had touched anything other than water. He was useless as an officer, and a bad influence on the men, and none of us doubted he would soon drink himself to death. So nobody was surprised - or particularly sorry - when he vanished one dark night when the sea was rough and the decks smashed down into every wave.

"Overboard," growled the captain, the next morning. "At least it saves us the trouble of finally putting him in irons."

The disappearance of Mr. Arrow left us a man short, but this wasn't a serious problem. Squire Trelawney had plenty of sailing experience and would stand a watch in calm weather. The coxswain, Israel Hands, took on some of the mate's duties. He was a wily, clever seaman who could be trusted with almost any job around the ship.

Hands spent all his free time with Long John Silver. The two seemed to be old friends. But then Silver was popular with the whole crew. I never discovered why they called him Barbecue, even though I spent hours listening to his stories of the sea and the strange lands he'd visited.

It was amazing to see him move around the ship, steadier and faster than most able-bodied men. He had some ropes strung across the deck which he used to pull himself around, even when the ship was rolling like the back of a galloping horse. Despite this, some of the old sailors pitied him for his missing limb.

"He's no ordinary man, our Barbecue," Hands told me one stormy night. "He had a real education, in school and everything, and can speak like a book when he wants. But he's brave too. A lion's nothing compared to Long John. With my own eyes I've seen him take on four men, unarmed, and knock them all down."

Silver was respected and obeyed by the whole crew. He had a way of making each man feel privileged to know him. With me, he was the kindest master, always glad to see me in his galley. He kept it neat and tidy, with all the dishes put away clean and his parrot hanging in a cage in the corner.

"Come and hear a story, Hawkins," he whispered, when the captain wasn't looking. "Nobody's more welcome than you in my galley, sonny. Sit down and hear the news. Here's Captain Flint, my parrot, named after the famous buccaneer. Here he is predicting a gentle voyage ahead of us."

"Pieces of eight!" screamed the parrot, right on cue.

"That bird," Silver explained, his eyes flashing, staring right into my own, "must be 200 years old. They live forever these tropical parrots, and nobody's seen more evil and wickedness than this one, except perhaps the Devil himself. She's sailed with pirate captains in every blood-stained cove in the Caribbean, and learned about treasure when she saw it torn out of Spanish galleons off Cape Horn, or plundered from warships in the wild Indian Ocean."

"Stand by to turn about," screamed the parrot.

He fed her pieces of sugar on the end of his finger and I watched in horror as the ancient bird pecked at the bars and let out a stream of foul, pirate oaths.

"You can't be around brimstone and not get stained, can you, lad?" Silver laughed. "She'd swear like that in front of a chaplain, the poor, innocent little thing."

He touched his cap with his finger in that strange salute of his, and I knew I was in the company of a fascinating man.

The squire and Captain Smollett, on the other hand, kept out of each other's way. The squire didn't hide the fact that he despised the captain, and Smollett never spoke unless asked a question and then his reply was always short, sharp and stern. He admitted to Livesey that he might have been wrong about the quality of the crew. As for the ship, he had grown fonder of her than any living person. "She's a beauty," he declared, "but we're still a long way from home and I don't like this cruise."

When he heard this, the squire marched off along the deck. "Any more of that man's impudence," he hissed, "and I will explode."

We had bouts of stormy weather, but the ship forged through it and the crew always seemed content. They had good cause - given that they were treated better than any sailors since the days of Noah and the great flood. The squire gave them double rum rations and sweet pudding on the slightest excuse, and there was always a fresh barrel of apples open below decks.

"We're spoiling them," Smollett complained to Livesey. "Spoil the hands and we'll turn them into devils."

But I was glad of those sweet apples as the days grew hot and sultry. And if it hadn't been for that open barrel, we might all have had our throats cut...

Inside the Barrel

We had picked up a strong trade wind and, as each hour brought us closer to our goal, the captain sent lookouts into the rigging. According to his charts, we would sight the island the following day, or sooner. While the *Hispaniola* cut a sharp wake over a quiet sea, everyone on board was full of excited anticipation, thrilled to be so close to Flint's old lair.

One evening after sundown, I was on my way to bed when I decided to go below decks and quench my thirst on a juicy apple. The watch crew were all at the prow of the ship, studying the horizon for any sight of land, so nobody saw me slip down the ladder. I padded over to the barrel in the middle of the storeroom and reached a hand in. But there were only a few fruits left, lying right at the bottom. The barrel came up to my chin, so I had to climb in and drop down to select an apple that wasn't too wormy or bruised. Sitting there in the dark, with the gentle slosh of the waves and the ship rocking like a cradle, I dozed off for a few seconds. Suddenly, the barrel rocked as a big man sat down against it, leaning his back against the staves. I heard a voice, Silver's, and was about to jump up and surprise him when he said something that made my blood run cold.

"Flint was the captain," snarled Long John, "not me. No, I was only the quartermaster, because of my peg leg. I lost it in a cannon broadside, the same blast that tore out old Pew's eyes. Flint hired a master surgeon to work on me, an educated fellow who could talk Latin when he wanted. They hanged him, of course, a month or two later, strung him up like a dog under a burning sun. He was from the *Royal Fortune*, an unlucky ship. On the *Walrus* we had the devil's luck, even when the decks were greasy with blood and the hold bulged with gold."

"Flint was a great man," cried another man, admiringly. I recognized his voice as one of the squire's recruits, a sailor not much older than myself.

"They were brave as lions, those old captains," Silver laughed. "I sailed with Captain England first, then with Flint. That's my story, and here I am now, with almost three thousand pounds in savings.

Earning's easy, lad, holding onto it is the challenge. Look at Flint's old crew; most of them are on this ship and glad to get the food and lodging. They were begging in the streets only a month ago. Look at Old Pew, who should have known better. He went through twelve hundred pounds in one year after Flint died. Then he begged and stole, cut throats and starved for two years, until he was run down in the road."

"That's no life for me," the young sailor agreed.

"No life for a fool," Silver cried. "But you're young, and smart as paint. I can talk to you like a man."

I shuddered when I heard this flattery, because it made me see how easily I'd been charmed myself.

"A smart man, like you," Silver continued, "could succeed as a gentleman of fortune. It's a rough life, and you risk the hangman's noose, but you'll eat and drink like a king. And when the cruise is finished, you'll have hundreds of pounds in your pockets, not farthings. Most men turn to rum and gambling, and head back to sea with nothing but the shirts on their backs. I set a different course, and stored my money away. I'm fifty, lad, and after this cruise I'll retire and live like a gentleman. It's been a good life to me, and I started like you, a common sailor in the forecastle."

"But you can't go back to Bristol," cried the other man. "Your inn and all your savings are gone."

"My missus has all the money," Silver chuckled. "I've sold the inn and she's sailing to meet me. I can't tell you where, even though I trust you, because the other men might want to know."

"Can you trust her?"

"Gentlemen of fortune," Silver purred, "are not usually the trusting kind. But I'm different. No man, or woman, cheats old John and lives to brag about it. Some men feared Pew, the braver ones feared Flint. But Flint himself was scared of me. The devil himself was too frightened to go to sea with Flint's crew, but when I was quartermaster they cowered before me. Nobody cheats Barbecue."

"Well John," cried the sailor. "I was nervous about this business before we had this talk, but I'm settled on it now. Let's shake on it."

"You're brave and smart," chuckled Silver.

I heard another man on the stairs and shrank even deeper into my barrel hideaway.

"Dick's joined us," declared Silver.

"I knew he would," coughed the voice of Israel Hands. "He's no fool." I heard him spit and rub his hands. "So now that's agreed, when do we strike, Barbecue? I've had my fill of that Captain Smollett. I want to get into their cabin, drink their wines and pick my teeth on their fine food."

"Wait, Israel," said Silver. "Your head's not much use for thinking, but you've got ears so listen. You'll sleep in the dripping prow and work hard, keep quiet and sober until I give the order."

"But when's that, Silver?"

"When, you want to know?" roared Silver angrily. "At the last possible moment. Smollett pilots the ship for us and the squire or doctor holds the map. Let them do all the work of finding the treasure, and helping us get it aboard. Then we can strike. If I could really trust you and the others, I'd have Smollett sail us half way home before we lifted a sword."

"We don't need him to work the ship," replied Hands.

"We can steer a course, but we can't plot one. Smollett could find the trade winds for us, but we'll have to take our chances of getting lost because you're not patient men like me. So, once the treasure's aboard, we'll finish them. You swabs are never happy until you're drunk and soaked in blood. Always in a hurry. And where does it end? On Execution Dock, that's where, hanging in the wind. If you would only bide your time until we were on a safe course for home, you could ride in a carriage like a lord. But no, you want rum tomorrow and the rest can go hang."

"But what will happen to the captain and the others?" Dick interrupted.

"What do you suggest?" asked Silver slyly. "We could maroon them, or slice them up like pork ribs."

"That was Billy Bones' style," laughed Hands. "He always said, *dead men don't bite*. He was a stone-hearted killer that sailor."

"I'm a gentleman compared to Billy," said Silver. "But I still say, death to them. When I'm riding in my coach I don't want some face from the past disturbing me. We must be patient. But, when we strike, we spare nobody."

"That's my man," growled Hands.

"And the squire's mine," hissed Silver. "I'll tear his head off with my bare hands. Now Dick, I'm all parched. Jump up and fetch me an apple."

If I was cold with fear before, it was nothing compared to the terror I experienced on hearing these words. I heard Dick rising from his stool, then Hands stopped him with a shout: "Let's have rum, Silver, if you're thirsty."

"Take my key, Dick," said Silver. "Fill us a jug. I trust you, of course, but remember I always mark the level on the keg."

Even in my terror, I wondered if this was how Mr. Arrow got hold of his drink? The thought seemed to clear my mind, and I forced myself to consider everything I'd heard. Dick had been offered a life of piracy with Silver's gang, and accepted. But were there any honest sailors left on board? The question was answered for me, when Hands barked out: "Not one more will join us."

When Dick returned, I heard the buccaneers slurping at their tin cups.

"To luck," cried Dick.

"To old man Flint," hissed Hands.

"To us," said Silver. "Be patient now and rich later."

The next instant, the ship turned suddenly, and my barrel filled with moonlight, flooding through the open hatchway to the top deck.

"Land ho," came a shout from the rigging.

The War Council

I could hear men rushing around the decks and sounds of commotion all around. When I was sure Silver and his friends had climbed the steps, I hauled myself out of the barrel, followed the passageway to the stern of the ship, and met Hunter and Dr. Livesey rushing to the top deck.

I joined them, peering over the bow. In the moonlight I saw two low hills poking out of a long bank of sea fog. Between them stood a third hill, but its peak was so high it was lost in the clouds. Captain Smollett adjusted his course so we would strike the island to the east, then gathered the men.

"Have any of you seen this land before?" he asked.

"I have, sir," answered Silver, who was standing at the heart of the throng. "I stopped there for water with a trading ship once."

"The best anchorage appears to be off an islet in the south," replied Smollett. "Is that correct?"

"Skeleton Island, they call it," answered Silver. "Pirates used to meet there, I believe. If the stories I've heard are true, the tall hill in the clouds is known as the Spyglass. They had look-outs there to keep an eye out for their hunters, and their prey."

"I have a map here," said Smollett. "Can you tell me if it's accurate?"

Long John's eyes flashed with greed as he snatched the chart, but he was disappointed. The doctor had made a copy of Billy Bones' map, complete in every detail, except the written instructions and the crosses showing where Flint's treasure was buried.

"All accurate," Silver sighed, concealing his frustration, "and very cleverly drawn. I wonder who could have made it?"

"Thank you, Silver," replied the captain, and he turned back to speak to the squire and the doctor. When I saw Silver sidling up to me through the crowd, I felt like screaming. But I controlled my fear. Even so, I shuddered when he laid one of his great fists on my shoulder.

"Jim," he whispered, "this is a sweet spot, this island. You can swim and climb trees, hunt goats and climb the steep cliff paths like a goat yourself. It makes me feel young again, being here. It's good to be young and have all your ten toes, believe me. When you want to go off exploring, just ask old John, and I'll get the boat ready to take you to shore."

He leered at me, then hurried off to talk with the milling sailors. I desperately wanted to interrupt the conference between my friends, to tell them everything I knew. But I didn't dare draw attention to myself. So I waited until the doctor called me over to fetch his pipe from the cabin, then tugged his coat sleeve.

"Get the captain and squire to the cabin," I whispered, leaning close to his chest. "Then send for me. I have terrible news."

The doctor's eyes sparkled for a second, but he calmed himself. "Thank you, Jim," he said loudly.

"That's all I wanted to know," he continued, pretending he'd called me over to ask something.

My friends went on talking for some minutes, until Captain Smollett suddenly called: "All hands on deck!" When the men were assembled, he lifted an arm to signal quiet.

"My lads," he began, "we've reached our destination, and you've all done the ship proud with your hard work. While the squire, the doctor and I go down to our cabin to drink your health, we want you to drink ours with a double measure of rum. Rum for all hands, and let's have a cheer for it."

The whole ship erupted in a mighty cheer to our good health. I could hardly believe these were the same men who were plotting to murder us.

"Let's have a cheer for Captain Smollett," boomed Long John, and the men obeyed. My friends went below and sent for me a few minute's later, while all the sailors were still sucking the last drops of rum from their tin cups.

The three men were seated at a table, with a bottle of Spanish wine and a bowl of raisins. Doctor Livesey had removed his wig in the heat of the evening, and was puffing nervously at his pipe.

"Let's hear it, Hawkins," the squire commanded. I repeated every word of the conversation I'd heard in the barrel. They were silent until I'd finished.

"Take a seat," said the doctor. They poured me a glass of wine, filled my palm with sweet raisins, then drank my good health and thanked me for my courage.

"Captain," said the squire, "you were right and I was wrong. I've been nothing but a fool. I am ready to obey your orders."

"You're no more a fool than I am, sir," replied the captain. "The men haven't given any signs of planning to mutiny. I've been tricked too."

"You can thank Silver for that," said the doctor. "He is no ordinary man."

"I'd like to see him swinging from an ordinary rope," cried the captain. "But we're wasting time. Allow me to outline our predicament, and propose a plan of action."

"Go on, captain," said the squire.

"We must behave as before," Smollett began. "If I ordered them to turn us about they'd mutiny at once. But we have some time to play with - at least until the treasure is located. And there are still some faithful hands who might help us. I suggest we take the fight to the pirates, pick our moment and surprise them with a sudden attack. Can we count on your servants, squire?"

"As you can count on me," declared Trelawney.

"That makes us seven, including Hawkins," said the captain. "We need to find the honest men in the crew."

"They'll be among the men Trelawney hired," the doctor suggested.

"But I chose Hands," the squire replied grimly.

"Yes," added the captain, "I had thought we could trust him."

"And to think they're all Englishmen," the squire protested, shaking his head.

"Well, sir," the captain responded, "at least seven of the twenty-six people aboard this ship are good Englishmen. We must be patient, and see if we can find some others."

On Dry Land

When I came on deck the next morning, I could see the eastern coast of the island lying only half a mile away across the waves. The isle was covered in grey woods, with streaks of sand in the lowlands and a few giant pine trees jutting out from the forest canopy. Above the trees, I noticed the bare rock hills were all oddly shaped. Towering above its escorts, the Spyglass had sheer sides, rising up to a plateau so smooth it looked like a table top.

While I surveyed the island, the *Hispaniola* rolled and dipped on the ocean swell. With the whole ship creaking and groaning, I had to grip the guide ropes to keep my balance, and even though I thought of myself as a good sailor, I felt my stomach knot with seasickness. I don't know if it was this nausea, or the sight of the island's dark, gloomy woods and wild stone spires that depressed me? But everything about the place made my heart sink: the surf pounding along the beach, the screech of shore birds and the blazing sun overhead.

I already hated the very thought of Treasure Island.

That day began with the dreary task of towing the ship to its anchorage between Skeleton Island and the shore, because there was no wind for her sails. I volunteered to help in one of the boats, and was surprised by how fiercely the men grumbled at their oars. They had been quick and cheerful sailors until we sighted Treasure Island.

Silver stood next to the man at the ship's wheel, helping to guide him through the narrow sea passage. He knew the channel like the back of his hand and piloted us exactly to where an anchor was marked on the map. We were about a third of a mile from the shore, bobbing in calm water with the grim forest surrounding us on three sides. I could make out a couple of swampy river mouths, where the plants grew with a poisonous brightness. There was no sign of any house, or the stockade that we knew from the chart was hidden among the trees. For all we could see, we might have been the only men to stop there since the island first bubbled up from the seabed.

There was not a breath of air, and no sound other than the surf. A peculiar, stagnant smell overcame the ship, a smell of rotting leaves and decay. I noticed the doctor sniffing at the air, like someone inspecting a bad egg.

"There's fever here," he declared. "I'd stake my wig on it."

I'd been alarmed by how angry the men seemed when I joined them in the boats, but when they returned to the ship they were in an even worse temper. They swore when they received the slightest order, and only grudgingly obeyed. Mutiny, it was clear, hung over us like a storm cloud. Only Long John Silver seemed cheerful and ready to do his duty. He moved among the sulking men, encouraging them with bursts of song and an anxious smile. Once the ship was secure, the captain called my friends and me to his cabin for another war council.

"If I give one more order," the captain began, "the whole ship will revolt. There's only one man who can help us."

"Who, sir?" asked the squire.

"Silver," the captain replied. "He doesn't want anything to happen to us yet. Let's give him a chance to settle the crew. We'll send them ashore for some rest. If they all go, we'll defend the ship, and if they refuse, we'll defend this cabin. But, if only some of them go, I'm certain that Silver will talk them round and buy us more time. He wants us to find the treasure before he cuts our throats."

After explaining the situation to the squire's three servants, the captain distributed pistols to us all in the cabin, then went on deck to address the crew.

"My lads," he called out, "it's been a hot day and you've worked hard. The boats are still in the water and you're all welcome to go ashore for the afternoon. I'll fire a gun before sundown as a signal to return."

The sailors started cheering and stamping on the ship's planks, startling the birds out of their forest nests. Captain Smollett shrewdly slipped below, leaving Silver to organize the landing parties. He arranged for six men to stay on board, while the rest of the crew, including himself, got ready to go ashore.

It was then that I had the first of the mad impulses that would help to save our lives. Making sure that nobody was watching, I slipped over the side and hid

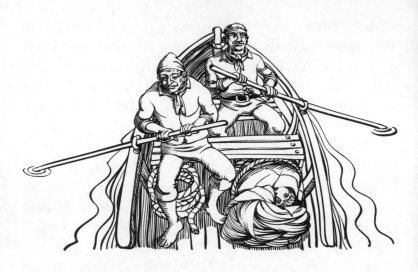

myself under a sail in the prow of one of the boats. With six sailors still on board, it would be difficult for us to take control of the ship and escape, but on the island I might learn something to our advantage.

We were halfway to shore when Silver spotted me from the other boat. "Is that you, Jim?" he cried over the water, but I ignored him. A few minutes later we slid onto a sandy beach and I wasted no time jumping out and dashing for the treeline.

"Jim, come back," I heard Silver cry behind me. But I didn't wait to answer him. I ran straight into the forest, until I could run no more.

With my lungs bursting for air, I came out into a sandy clearing, dotted with pines and stunted, twisted trees. For the first time since I'd seen the island, I felt a surge of excitement. I was an explorer, with nothing in front of me but strange plants, dumb brutes and exotic birds. I wandered between the trees, stepping around clumps of garish flowers. Here and there I saw snakes. One lifted his head from a low ledge of rock and hissed at me, filling the air with a strange crackling noise. Only later I discovered this was a rattlesnake, and deadly poisonous.

I came to a thick grove of evergreen oaks, their branches twisting across the sand like brambles. Beyond the oaks I could see one of the swampy river mouths that ran into the bay, covered in mist where the sun warmed the ground. There was a sudden bustle and squawk as a wild duck burst out of the trees. The next moment, the air was full of screeching, frightened birds. I guessed some of the crew must be approaching the swamp and had disturbed them. Soon, I could make out the low rumble of human voices, growing louder and nearer.

I crawled under one of the oak trees and hid. It was Silver and another man. I was terrified that they might stumble across me. But, crouching at the base of the tree, I soon began cursing my cowardice. This was an opportunity to learn something that might help us - and here was I, hiding like a frightened mouse. I started crawling towards the sound of their voices.

I stopped on top of a bank of ferns and peered through the leaves. The two men were below me in a little clearing, face to face in conversation. Silver had thrown his hat on the ground beside him, and his great, smooth face was glistening with sweat in the morning sun. He lifted his eyes to the other man with a look of kind concern.

"Mate," he said softly, "it's only because I respect you that we're having this little chat. What's done is done. You can't change it. Tom, I'm trying to protect you from the wild ones."

"Silver," cried the other man, his voice tight with rage, "you're old and you're honest, so I hear. You've got money and you're brave too. So why are you running with this pack of mutinous dogs? I'd rather lose my head than be a traitor to my captain."

There was a sudden cry from deep in the forest, followed by a terrible, drawn-out scream. It echoed around the hills until the whole flock of marsh birds rose again in a great cloud of flapping bodies. Finally, the scream faded, and only the rustle of the returning birds and the distant, grinding surf disturbed the silence of the clearing.

Silver didn't blink an eye. He rested on his crutch, watching the other man like a snake about to spring.

"Barbecue," Tom pleaded, reaching out a hand.

"Hands off," roared Silver, leaping backwards as nimbly as a gymnast.

"Tell me, what was that?" cried the man, still trying to touch Silver like a drowning man pleading for help.

"Oh, that?" said Silver, his eyes as still and cold as shards of glass. "That must be Alan."

"Alan?" Tom cried in a sudden fury. "Then bless his soul, he was a true seaman. You've been a mate of mine, Silver, but no longer. If I die, I'll die doing my duty, like Alan. Kill me too, if you can. But I'm turning you down."

This brave man turned his back on the cook and

started walking towards the beach. Silver screamed in rage, grabbed the branch of a tree for support and hurled his crutch like a heavy javelin. It struck Tom point first in the middle of his back. The poor sailor gasped and fell forwards.

From the sound of the impact, I guessed the crutch had snapped Tom's back and he was dead before he hit the ground. But Silver was taking no chances. He sprang across the clearing like a monkey, and the next instant was on top of the sailor and had buried his knife in his motionless body. I was so close, I could hear him pant aloud as he jabbed at the corpse.

The murderer cleaned his knife on some tufts of grass, collected his hat and crutch, then calmly took a whistle from his pocket and blew a high note several times. My mind racing with all I'd just seen, I realized the danger I was in. The rest of the pirate gang would be rushing to answer this signal, thrashing through the ferns and clambering around the trees towards me. I had to escape. Backing away from the ledge, I heard a chorus of wild calls and shouts erupt from the forest. They were close already. Once I had skirted the oaks in the swamp, I started running, directionless and almost blind with fear, until my legs could hardly move. But at least I was away from the pirates and out of immediate danger. When I had recovered enough strength to lift my head and look around, I almost jumped in fright. I saw a flicker, a dark, threatening shape, darting between the trees ahead.

I couldn't tell what kind of beast it was: a bear, monkey or man. But the sight filled me with terror. I started retracing my steps through the forest, less afraid of Silver and his men than of this phantom creature. But I noticed the shape flitting from trunk to trunk to cut off my retreat. It was running stooped over on two legs and I could see it was some kind of a man - but unlike any man I'd seen before. I tried to recall all the stories I'd heard about savages and cannibals, wondering if there was some way I could protect myself. Then I remembered the pistol in my pocket, and felt a rush of courage. I advanced boldly towards the wild man.

I saw a dark face studying me from behind a tree trunk. As I approached he stepped out into the light, then hesitated, before finally throwing himself down on his hands and knees.

"Who are you?" I cried.

"Ben Gunn," the creature replied, his voice hoarse and dry like a rusty lock. "Poor Ben Gunn who hasn't spoken with a civilized man for three whole years."

His skin - even his lips - was so worn by long exposure to the sun it was almost black. With his big, fair eyes, he had a startling face, almost handsome. But he was the scruffiest specimen of mankind I had ever encountered, clothed in a crazy patchwork of hide, torn cloth, ship's canvas and rags held together by string and bits of twigs.

"Were you shipwrecked?" I asked.

"No, mate," he chuckled. "Marooned."

This was one of the worst punishments for a sailor - abandoned on some desolate island, alone and without tools or supplies except for a loaded pistol. Madness or despair drove most to shoot themselves.

"I've lived on goats, berries and oysters for three years," Ben Gunn told me. "A man can survive anywhere, but there are things he misses. You don't happen to have a piece of cheese on you?" He eyed me greedily. "I've had so many dreams about cheese, toasted mostly - and then woken up on this rock."

"If I ever get back to my ship," I promised, "I'll give you cheese by the stone."

Throughout our conversation he had been smiling, stroking my clothes and fawning over me as though he could hardly believe I was real. But he suddenly shot me a sly glance.

"What's stopping you from getting to your ship?" he asked. "And what's your name, mate, come to that?"

"Jim."

"I was a good boy growing up, Jim, though you wouldn't believe it to look at me now. My troubles began with the silly games boys play, gambling for pennies, until I got a taste for it. My mother told me how it would end, and she was right. God's will put me in this place, so I could reflect on my sins. And I have. I'll be a good man from now, won't even touch rum, except a thimbleful for luck the first chance I get. But I'm going to lead a good life. And Jim," he whispered, looking all around, "I'm rich, you know?"

He must have guessed from my expression that I thought the years of solitude had driven him mad, because he squealed and raised his hands in protest. "I am, I am," he cried. "And I'll make you rich too, Jim, for being the first man to find me." Glancing around again, he was suddenly furtive. "Now, Jim," he hissed, "that isn't Flint's ship in the bay, is it?"

"No, Flint's dead," I answered quickly, wondering if I'd found an unexpected ally in Ben Gunn. "But some of his men are on board, worse luck for the rest of us."

"Is there a man there," he whispered, "with one leg?"

"Silver?" I cried. "He's the cook and ringleader."

Ben Gunn snatched at my wrist, making me flinch.

"If Long John sent you," he cried, "I'm dead meat. But I'll make sure of you first."

I quickly explained how I had come to the island, and the danger my friends were in.

When I'd finished, he patted me on the head. "You're a good lad, Jim," he laughed, "in a tight spot. But you can trust old Ben. Is the squire reasonable?"

"Of course."

"He wouldn't mind parting with... let's say a thousand pounds of what he hopes to find, and a passage home for poor Ben Gunn?"

"The squire's a gentlemen," I cried. "All hands would get a fair share, and we could use some help working the ship."

"Right then," he whispered, looking relieved, "I'll tell you my story. I was here with Flint when he went off with six strong men and a chest of gold. They were gone a week, while we waited on the *Walrus*. At last, Flint comes back alone, with a scarf fixed around his bleeding head, his face as white as salt. But he was still standing. He'd killed the other six, though none of us discovered how. Of course Billy Bones and Silver wanted to know where the treasure was. But Flint just laughed. 'Go ashore, then, and stay there. But the *Walrus* is setting sail now.'

"So I came back to the island three years ago, on another ship. 'There's treasure here, boys,' I told the crew. We dug for twelve days, and each day they hated me more. On the thirteenth day, they returned to the ship. 'As for you, Benjamin Gunn, they said, 'here's a gun and a spade. You can spend the rest of your life digging.' And then they sailed away"

Then he pinched my wrist and winked a few times. "But there's more to me than just a simple sailor, Jim, much more. You tell the squire Ben Gunn's the man for him, and that he'll put more confidence in a born gentleman than he does in any gentlemen of fortune, having tried that way of life himself."

"I don't understand a word you've said," I told him, "but it doesn't matter anyway because I can't get back to the ship."

"But I have a boat," he whooped in excitement. "I made her myself and keep her hidden below the white rock. She's hard to handle, until you learn her habits, but we could take her out to your ship after dark."

Suddenly we pricked up our ears - the boom of a cannon thundered around the three hills of Treasure Island.

"The fighting's started," I shouted. "Follow me."

I started racing towards the shoreline, with Ben Gunn loping alongside. He kept up easily, babbling away as we tore through the forest. I heard a volley of rifle shots and came to an opening in the trees. A Union Jack flag fluttered and rippled above the forest canopy, only a few hundred yards from where we stood.

The Doctor Takes Over

At this point in my story, I will 'pass the pen' to Dr. Livesey, so he may describe what happened on board the *Hispaniola* during my absence. He has kindly sent this letter, which contains all the vital facts:

If I may say so, Jim, you've done a fine job with this yarn so far. I hope my note can fill any gaps in your account of the adventure. Well, we would have attacked the six mutineers Silver left on board but for two reasons: there wasn't enough wind for us to escape to the open sea and Hunter broke the news that Jim had gone ashore in one of the boats. The way the crew had behaved that morning, I wondered if I'd ever see Jim again. From the top deck I stared into the green, swampy forest, looking for some sign of my friend. I could almost smell the fever and sickness that festered on that island.

"I'm going ashore," I told the squire. "We've got to find out what's going on."

Hunter and I set out in a small rowing boat, making for the direction of the stockade marked on Flint's map. We could see Silver's two boats, each with a single guard, beached at the mouth of the swamp. The two men jumped up and waved their arms when they saw us rowing past, but Silver must have ordered them to stay with the boats, whatever happened. If one of them had run into the forest to raise the alarm, our fate could have been very different.

When we reached the beach, I jumped out and charged into the forest, almost running straight into the perimeter fence around the stockade. Flint, or some other pirate captain, had done a good job of building this fort, which was positioned around a spring of clear water at the summit of a small knoll. The pirates had clapped together a stout log house around the spring. It had one room, big enough to hold forty men at a pinch, with slits for their rifles in each wall. There was a clearing of felled trees all around the fort, then an unbroken, six-foot high timber spike fence. Any attacker would have to climb the fence and rush across open ground to reach the log house, making themselves an easy target. If the defenders had enough food and a sharp-eyed man on watch, they could hold this place against a whole regiment.

The spring was a sight for sore eyes. We had plenty of food, arms and excellent wines on the Hispaniola, but no fresh water. I was smiling about my discovery when I heard the unmistakable scream of someone in their death-throes echoing around the island. I'm no stranger to the horrors of the battlefield, but I admit my heart missed a beat when I heard that scream. "Jim Hawkins is gone," was my first thought.

But doctors cannot afford to let their feelings delay their actions. I recovered my composure and ran back to shore, where Hunter was waiting to row us back to the ship. He pulls a good oar and we were soon clambering aboard. The first thing I saw was the squire, his face white as chalk.

"I'm to blame," he whispered. "I brought us to this terrible place."

"Never mind the squire," Smollett quickly hissed in my ear. "One of the sailors almost fainted when he heard that scream. He must be new to this kind of work, and might be willing to join us. Now what's your plan, doctor?"

Redruth took up guard in the passageway between the cabin and the forecastle, armed with four loaded muskets and shielded by a mattress. Hunter brought the rowing boat around to the stern and Joyce and I started loading gunpowder, biscuits, legs of pork, a cask of cognac and my invaluable medicine bag. While we prepared the escape craft, the captain approached Israel Hands, the leader of the sailors left on board with us.

"Mr. Hands," announced the captain icily, "we have four pistols between us and if any man tries to make a signal we'll shoot him dead."

The whole group rushed down one of the hatches, thinking they could get behind us along the passageway. When they saw Redruth waiting for them, they tried to climb back onto deck.

"Down, you dogs," the captain ordered.

While the squire and captain kept watch over the six sailors, Hunter, Joyce and I returned to the stockade with the first load of supplies. I saw one of the pirates scamper into the forest, and guessed we had no time to waste. We threw the supplies over the stockade fence and I left Joyce and Hunter to guard them while I rowed back to the Hispaniola, summoning up all my strength.

The squire was waiting for me at the cabin porthole, and I was heartened to see his expression was fiercer and more determined than ever. We loaded the boat with *more supplies, taking three muskets and cutlasses for Redruth, the captain, the squire and myself. I dropped the remaining weapons into the sea, and allowed myself a grin when I saw the bright steel glinting far below.*

At last, we were ready to make the run to shore. The captain rushed over to the hatch to the forecastle.

"I'm speaking to you, Abraham Gray," he called. "I order you to follow your captain off this ship. I know you're a good man at heart, so you have thirty seconds to join us."

There was a shout below, a scuffle and sound of blows, then Abraham Gray burst into the bright sunlight with a fresh cut in his cheek. "I'm with you, sir," he cried.

The next instant we were all crowded into the boat, racing for the shore. We were badly overloaded, and before we'd made one hundred yards my trousers and coat-tails were sodden. But this was the least of our worries. The tide had turned and our little boat was being carried towards the beach where Silver's men had landed. I struggled with the rudder, but the current was too strong.

"We should be able to row through it," said Gray. But Smollett's eyes had turned back to the Hispaniola.

"The gun," he whispered, almost to himself. "We've forgotten the gun."

I glanced behind and saw the five figures struggling with the covers of the cannon mounted by the main mast. We hadn't thought of sinking the powder or balls for this weapon - they were still in the cabin.

"Hands was Flint's gunner," said Gray, hoarsely.

"Keep rowing," the captain ordered. "Who's the best shot in this boat."

"*Mr. Trelawney,*" I replied.

"*Squire,*" said the captain calmly, "*will you please fire at one of those pirates on board. That rascal, Hands, if possible.*"

I watched the squire load his musket with a grip as steady as steel. Hands was at the muzzle of the cannon, ramming home some powder. But, at the same second Trelawney fired, Hands ducked down to pick something from the deck. One of the other men around the gun howled in pain and toppled over.

The next instant I heard a roar of voices from the beach and turned to see a gang of pirates trooping out from between the trees and taking their places in a boat.

"Here they come," I cried. "They're sending one boat after us. The other men are working their way along the shore to the stockade."

"We'll be there before them," the captain responded confidently. "It's the gun that's the danger."

I could see Hands working furiously to get the cannon loaded. He and the others hadn't even looked at the wounded man, and I could see him trying to crawl away along the deck.

"They're firing," cried the squire.

We yanked on the oars to try to turn the boat. Then I heard a crunch and a boom and felt the cannon ball whistle over our heads. Hands had missed, but we were sinking. The boat was too heavy for the sudden movement, and we sank in three feet of water, only yards from the beach. All the stores were gone.

"Save what you can," shouted the captain. "Wade ashore and make for the stockade."

I could already hear the shouts of our pursuers, ringing through the woods. Soon, I could hear their running feet and the sound of branches cracking as they pushed through the trees.

"Give Trelawney your musket, sir," I advised the captain. "Mine is underwater and he is the best shot."

The squire, as silent and cool as he had been in the boat, checked the weapon. Meantime, I noticed Gray was unarmed so I gave him my cutlass. When he spat in his hands and made a few sword strokes through the air, we felt braver. Gray was clearly worth his salt in any battle.

We reached the stockade fence on the south side, and saw seven of the crew rush around the southwestern corner. They paused in surprise at the sight of us, and we managed to get off four shots - including two from the blockhouse - before they knew what was happening. The *pirates plunged into the forest leaving one man on the ground, shot through the heart.*

We were smiling over our easy victory when I heard a crack from the treeline and saw poor Tom Redruth tumble over. From a glance I could see he was finished, but we carried him over the fence groaning and bleeding. He'd never complained once, this loyal servant, despite all the dangers we'd put him through. We laid him down gently in the log cabin, and the squire dropped down next to him, blubbing like a child.

"Am I going, doctor?" Tom asked me.

"You're going home," I replied.

"I wish I'd had a shot at them first," he groaned.

"Tom, say you forgive me," begged the squire.

"I don't know if that's proper," whispered Tom, "between a servant and squire. But I do, of course. Could someone read a prayer," he asked. Soon after, he was dead.

When I had finished tending to the dying man, I came out into the enclosure and saw the captain struggling with a long pole he'd found. He fixed it to the side of the cabin, climbed onto the roof and ran up a Union Jack flag he had hidden in his tunic. I saw a proud look flash across his face, before he bounded down to join me. "Dr. Livesey," he asked, "when do you and the squire expect Blandly's ship to come looking for us?"

"Not for months," I answered.

"A pity," he said, scratching his head. "We're well-armed but our food supplies are low. Perhaps it's just as well we've one less mouth to feed."

He pointed to where Tom's body lay covered. Before I could reply there was a whistle and the air shook as a cannonball passed over the roof of the cabin and drilled into the forest canopy.

"Blaze away," roared the captain in defiance. "You're wasting your powder, Hands."

The next shot landed inside the enclosure, sending up a cloud of sand as it thudded to earth.

"Captain," said the squire, frowning, "you can't see the stockade from the ship. The rogues must be aiming at your flag. Wouldn't it be wiser to lower it?"

"Strike my flag?" cried the captain. "Never, sir."

All through the evening they kept thundering away at us. But they were too far away to do any real damage, and even when a ball popped through the roof of the cabin we managed to laugh about it.

"We've got rations for ten days," the captain finally announced, after carefully checking our stores. "There are six of us, to bear arms. One man is dead, and one cabin boy is missing."

There was a shout from Hunter, who was standing watch outside. "Somebody's hailing us, sir," he cried. "I think he's climbing the fence."

We all ran out into the enclosure, weapons at the ready. Jim Hawkins was dropping down from the perimeter wall, running towards us, a broad smile across his face.

Back to you now, Jim...

David Livesey, MD

Cutlass and Pistol

When Ben Gunn saw the Union Jack he knew my friends had taken the fort.

"No self-respecting pirate would fly that flag," he assured me. "Silver would choose the Jolly Roger. There's been a fight, I'll bet, and your friends are safe in Flint's old fort. It's a real stronghold that place."

"If they're trapped in the fort," I replied, "I must join them."

"You can go alone," he whispered. "It's no place for Ben Gunn. But you know where to find me, when you want me. Send one of your friends, Jim, and tell them to come alone, carrying a white cloth. It'll be to their advantage, you might say."

"I understand," I snapped, anxious to be on my way. "Is that all?"

"They've a lot to gain," he continued mysteriously, "and everything to lose on this island. Ben Gunn's the man to help them. One more thing, Jim," he added, snatching at my hand. "If you happened to meet Silver, you wouldn't mention Ben Gunn to him, would you? Even under torture, you wouldn't say a word?"

"Of course not," I replied.

"I know you wouldn't, lad. You won't tell on Ben Gunn. You see, if those pirates camp ashore tonight, there'll be some new widows in the morning."

Before I could ask him what he was talking about, a cannonball pitched into the sand only a few yards from where we were standing. When I had rubbed the dust out of my eyes, the wild man had vanished into the trees.

It took me several hours to work my way through the forest, wary of pirate patrols and the sudden, terrifying whistle of the cannonballs. When I came to a clearing, I spotted the *Hispaniola* lying at anchor out in the bay. Just as Ben Gunn had predicted, the grim image of the Jolly Roger was flapping at her mast.

Along the shore, a group of the pirates were hacking at the remains of the rowing boat with axes. They'd lit a great bonfire near the mouth of the river, and the trees flickered red and orange in the twilight gloom. I could hear their whoops and cries as they loped through the forest. There was a shrill excitement in their voices that made me suspect they'd cracked open Silver's barrel of rum.

As I turned to make my way towards the stockade, the last thing I noticed in the fading light was a crag of rock looming over the trees. It was close to the shore and as white as the moon, and I wondered if Ben Gunn's ramblings about a secret boat had been true. While I turned this question over in my mind, I stumbled into the rough stakes of the stockade.

My friends gave me a warm welcome, and listened carefully to every part of my adventure. While I talked, I looked around me at the blockhouse where we had taken refuge. It looked sturdy and well-provisioned, but the cold, evening breeze whistled through every

crack in its heavy, log walls, bringing with it a cloud of fine sand that had settled everywhere. We had sand in our eyes, in our teeth and in every mouthful of food we ate that night. As if that wasn't bad enough, my eyes were streaming with smoke. Our chimney was a square hole cut in the roof, and most of the smoke stayed inside, settling in a thick cloud at head-height.

But there was no time to stand around feeling sorry for ourselves. Captain Smollett saw to that. He divided us into two watches, sent two men out to scavenge for firewood and ordered two others to dig a grave for poor Redruth, whose body lay in a corner of the hut, covered with another Union Jack flag.

I was on guard duty at the door when the doctor approached. He'd been given the job of cook, but every now and again he had to leave the smoky interior for some fresh air.

"Jim," he whispered to me on one of his visits to the open door, "our captain is certainly a better man than I am."

I nodded. Captain Smollett had taken charge of us like a true leader of men. The doctor was silent for a moment, staring out into the night, lost in his thoughts.

"Is Ben Gunn sane?" he asked suddenly. "Or has he gone mad after three years of biting his nails on this island?"

"I couldn't tell you, sir," I answered.

"He asked for cheese?"

"Yes, sir."

"But mad or not, as a secret gourmet I might be able to help him," said the doctor mysteriously. "You've seen my snuff box, haven't you, Jim?"

"Of course, sir," I replied, puzzled.

"But you've never seen me take snuff, have you? The reason's simple. In my snuff box there is a piece of Parmesan cheese, Jim, and not a grain of snuff. That piece of delicious cheese is for Ben Gunn. Let's hope it wins him over to our cause."

We buried old Tom before we sat down for dinner, standing by his rough grave with our hats in our hands. After filing back into the blockhouse, the doctor doled out boiled pork and a cup of brandy to each man. After this feast, our three chiefs - the doctor, squire and captain - retired to a corner and discussed our chances of survival.

"Our stores are too low," whispered the captain. "They'll starve us into surrender, long before any rescue boat arrives."

"Then we'll have to fight," the squire responded

fiercely. "Their numbers are down to fifteen, two of whom are wounded."

"And there's the man you shot by the cannon," added the doctor. "I imagine he's buried by now."

"Then we'll pick them off slowly," the captain snapped. "Each time we trade shots we'll clip one more. The squire's musket will save us."

"We have two more weapons on our side," added the doctor, "rum and the swamp. Just listen to them out there."

I could hear the pirates roaring and singing down in the marshy glades by the shore. They had made their camp and were celebrating the mutiny.

"I'll stake my wig," the doctor continued, "that before the end of the week, half of them will be down with fever."

"We'll beat them in a fight," cried the squire, "or force them to sail away on the *Hispaniola*."

"It's the first ship I've lost," said the captain sadly.

It was the last I heard of their conversation. I was dead tired and couldn't keep my eyes open a moment longer. When I woke in the glaring light of the new day, I heard a shout and the sound of running feet.

"Two pirates," cried a voice. "And one of them's waving a white flag."

I dashed over to a gun-slit and spotted two men on the far side of the stockade fence. One pirate was waving a flag of surrender; the other was Long John Silver, looking as nonchalant as ever in the dim light of dawn.

It was the coldest morning I'd ever known, so cold it made my bones ache. The sky was bright and cloudless overhead, but down at the edge of the forest there was a low fog creeping up from the swamp. It curled around Silver and the other pirate, lapping at their waists.

"Load your guns and stay inside, men," the captain ordered. "Ten to one it's a trick to draw us into the open." He hailed Silver and his accomplice: "Keep your distance, or we open fire."

"This is a flag of peace," protested Silver.

"What use is it to you?" replied Smollett.

"Captain Silver's come to make terms, sir," called out the other pirate.

"*Captain* Silver?" Smollett laughed. "My, that was a quick promotion."

"It was the crew, sir," answered Silver meekly. "They elected me after your *desertion*. We'll leave you in peace, if we can agree on terms. I want your promise that we can have safe passage in and out of the stockade, so we can talk."

"I've nothing to say to you, Silver," the captain answered boldly. "But you can enter if you wish."

The old pirate tossed his crutch over the fence and swung himself over with the grace of a cat. He was less agile climbing the hill up to the blockhouse: the steep incline and soft sand were difficult terrain for his crutch. When he finally reached the doorway, he saluted Smollett proudly, as though they were two captains meeting at sea. Silver almost looked the part. He had swapped his rough clothes for a fine blue coat dotted with brass buttons, and he wore a lace hat. Smollett didn't return the salute, but settled himself down on a stool in the doorway of the blockhouse.

"Well, Silver," he said, "you'd better sit down too."

"Out here on the sand, sir?" complained Long John. "Won't you invite me inside?"

"If you were an honest man," replied Smollett, "you'd still be sitting in the ship's galley. Make your choice. You're either my cook, and deserve my respect, or you're a mutineer and pirate and you can go hang."

"I'll sit," grumbled Silver, "but I'll need a hand up later. Well, you've made yourselves comfortable, I see," he told us, peering into the shadows of the blockhouse interior. "Top of the morning to you, Jim. Hello Doctor. Here you all are like one big happy family, in a manner of speaking."

"What do you want, Silver?" the captain snapped.

"Back to business so quickly," sighed Long John. "Well, that was a fancy trick of yours last night. One of you is a good man with a club, I'll concede, and some of my people were badly shaken by it. But don't try it again, by thunder," he suddenly snarled, his voice changing in an instant from the usual, gentle purr. "I wasn't drunk like the others, and if I'd woken a second sooner I would have caught you in the act. He was still alive when I reached him."

"Is that all?" asked the captain, showing no surprise, although I guessed he was as puzzled as the rest of us by Silver's speech. Had Ben Gunn killed a pirate in the dark, I wondered? If so, the enemy was down to fourteen men.

"The members of the crew are a dangerous and unpredictable crowd," said Silver, softly. "They want the treasure, and will do anything to get it. You want to stay alive. Now, we can each have what we desire, if you'll only give Long John the map. There'll be violence otherwise, and I never wanted that."

"We know what you were plotting," answered the captain, and he calmly began filling his pipe while Silver's face turned scarlet with rage.

"What lies has Gray told you?" he roared.

"Stop there," cried Smollett. "Gray's said nothing."

"So you say," replied Silver. "Perhaps I'll join you in taking a pipe."

For the next twenty minutes, the two men faced each other on the sand, each puffing at his pipe and studying his opponent. It was Silver who finally broke the silence.

"Here are my terms," he began. "You give us the map, and stop shooting poor seamen and stoving in their heads while they sleep. If you do that, I'll offer you a choice. Come with us in the *Hispaniola* once the treasure's loaded, and I'll drop you at a safe port. I give you my word as a gentleman of fortune on it. Or, if you prefer to stay here, I'll give you stores and send the first ship I sight to fetch you. That's a rare deal for you, don't you think so, Captain Smollett?"

Smollett stood up and knocked the ashes from his pipe into his palm. "Is that all?"

"If you refuse," replied Silver sharply, "you've seen the last of me but musket-balls."

"Then hear me," cried the captain. "Give yourselves

110

up, and I'll take you home to a fair trial in England. If not, my name is Alexander Smollett, I've hoisted my king's flag and I'll see you in hell before I surrender. You can't find the treasure. You can't navigate the ship and you can't outfight us. You're trapped in a dead calm sea with a rabble crew, *captain* Silver, and the next time we meet I'll put a bullet in your belly. Be off with you, lad. Get going, on the double."

Silver's whole face twitched with fury and his eyes flashed like lightning.

"Who'll help me up?" he cried.

"Not I," answered Smollett. None of us moved.

The old pirate let out a stream of vile oaths that made me shudder. He dragged himself over to the porch and pulled himself up, snatching for his crutch.

"See that?" he roared, spitting into the sand. "That's what I think of you. I'll be inside your blockhouse within the hour. Laugh while you can. Those that die quickly will be the lucky ones."

He stumbled down the hill away from us, cursing with every step.

"Man your posts," cried the captain, as soon as Silver had scrambled over the stockade and vanished into the trees. "He wasn't bragging, lads, we're in for a fight. We're outnumbered, but we've got the advantage of the fort. If we keep our nerve, we'll come out on top, I promise." He paced around the blockhouse, checking our guns and stores of ammunition. "Throw out the embers," he ordered. "We don't want smoke in our eyes. Hawkins, take some food for your breakfast, but you can eat it at your post. Hunter, fetch brandy for all hands."

While we sipped on the fiery liquid, Smollett gave us his final battle instructions.

"Doctor, you guard the door but keep well inside. Hunter, man the east gun-slit, Joyce the west. We must keep them away from the gun-slits, men, or they'll be shooting us like fish in a barrel. Squire, you're the marksman. You and Gray can guard the north wall with its five gun-slits. Hawkins and I are poor shots, so we can be loaders."

We waited nervously at our posts as the sun began to warm the clearing. Soon, the sand was baking and the resin was melting out of the logs. We threw off our jackets and coats and rolled up our shirt sleeves as the heat in the blockhouse became unbearable. An hour went by.

"Curse them," snapped the captain. "This is as dull as a month in the doldrums."

"Sir?" asked Joyce politely. "If I see one of them, should I open fire."

"Immediately," cried the captain.

"Thank you, sir," Joyce replied.

His words set us all on edge, straining our eyes and ears while the captain stood frowning in the middle of the blockhouse. Suddenly, Joyce took aim and fired. The next second my ears were ringing as a volley of shots broke out from every side of the stockade, like geese clacking. I heard several bullets hammer into the logs and then there was silence again. There was no sign of our enemies in the shadows of the forest.

"Did you hit him?" demanded Smollett.

"I don't think so, sir," Joyce answered.

"I respect your honesty," grumbled the captain. "Load his gun, Jim. How many guns on your side, doctor?"

"I saw three flashes," came the answer.

"Your side, Squire?"

"Between seven and nine guns," replied Trelawney. "I'd say the bulk of their force is there."

"I can't leave any wall undefended," cried the captain. "We must guard all the gun-slits."

There was no time to question his tactics. With a loud roar a band of pirates broke out of the trees on the north side and hurled themselves at the stockade. To support their charge, I heard gunshots from the woods all around us and a bullet sang through the doorway and smashed the doctor's musket to bits.

The pirates swarmed over the fence like monkeys, but I saw three of them knocked down by our guns. One of them staggered off into the trees, leaving four pirates inside the enclosure, armed with pistols and cutlasses. They sprinted towards us, screaming a war cry that was echoed by the pirates out in the forest. I recognized a man named Job Anderson among them. In an instant, he had reached the blockhouse and was shouting through one of the gun-slits:

"At 'em lads, cut 'em open."

Another pirate grabbed Hunter's rifle, turned the butt around and with one stunning blow laid poor Hunter on the ground. A third man appeared at the doorway and began hacking at the doctor with his cutlass.

"Out lads," cried the captain, "we'll fight them in the open."

I took a cutlass and charged into the daylight. The first thing I saw was the doctor, chasing after the pirate from the doorway. With one mighty slash of his cutlass he sent the man rolling down the hill.

"Round to the north side, lads," boomed the captain. I obeyed without thinking, rushing to the corner of the blockhouse and coming face to face with Job Anderson. He let out a scream and raised his rusty cutlass over his head so it glinted in the sun. There was no time to be afraid. I dodged to one side, lost my footing and rolled down the hill. When I turned I saw Gray plunge his cutlass into Anderson's chest. He writhed in agony, his pistol still smoking, while the only survivor from the raiding party was running towards the stockade. We had won.

"Back to the house," called the doctor. Gray helped me to my feet and we rushed back to shelter. Inside the dark room, I saw the price we had paid for our victory: Hunter was stretched out on the ground, stunned, and Joyce had been shot through the head. In the middle of the room, the squire was supporting the captain, their faces as pale as milk.

"The captain's wounded," said Mr. Trelawney.

"Have they run away?" Smollett asked.

"All that could," answered the doctor. "Five of them will never run again."

"Then the odds are improving," cried the captain cheerily. "Now we're only outnumbered two to one."

Aboard the Hispaniola

Out of the eight men who had fallen in the raid, only three of them were still breathing: the pirate who fell at the gun slit, Hunter and Captain Smollett. The pirate died while the doctor tended to his wounds, and poor Hunter's chest was so badly crushed he was as good as dead. Our captain had been shot twice by Anderson, in the shoulder and the calf. He was badly wounded, but the doctor told us he would recover in time. All he needed was total rest and careful treatment - conditions that would be hard to find on Treasure Island.

Silver's pirates must have been licking their wounds in the swamp, because we heard nothing from them all morning. After a dinner of pork and beans, the squire, Smollett and Doctor Livesey had a long, private discussion. It ended just after noon, with the doctor picking up his hat and two pistols and strapping a sword belt around his waist. He folded Flint's map carefully away in his pocket and with a musket over his shoulder he crossed the enclosure, climbed the stockade and set off briskly through the trees.

Gray was so thunderstruck by this sight he let his pipe slip from his mouth. "In the name of Davy Jones' locker," he gasped, "has the doctor gone mad?"

"I don't think so, sir," I replied. "I believe he's going to meet a certain Ben Gunn."

116

With every minute that passed, the sun seemed to burn hotter inside the stockade, and I began to envy the doctor, strolling through the cool glades of the forest. While I was being grilled by the fierce heat, surrounded by blood and dead bodies, he was listening to the birds and smelling the sweet pines and flowers. The longer I spent doing my chores, the more I wanted to escape into the fresh heart of the forest.

Passing a bag full of bread and biscuits, I found myself filling my pockets - supplies for another one of my rash adventures. Next, I took two pistols, and decided I was fully equipped for my mission. I wanted to find out if Ben Gunn was telling the truth about his boat at the White Rock. The captain would never give me permission to leave the stockade, so I would have to take *French leave*, and return before anyone noticed I was missing.

When Gray and the squire were changing the bandage on the captain's leg, I saw my chance. I made a bolt for it over the stockade, aiming for the thickest part of the forest. It was late afternoon when I left my friends. As I weaved between the huge trees I could hear the thunder of the surf and the music of the high branches waving in the sea breezes.

After a short hike I came out onto the shore and saw the *Hispaniola*, still anchored in the shelter of Skeleton Island. Although she was a mile offshore, I could make out a cluster of men laughing and talking in one of the boats, lashed along her side. Silver was among them. It was impossible to catch their words, but when I heard a horrid, unearthly scream my heart jumped - until I realized it was Silver's parrot, perched on her master's wrist.

I saw the boat head off for land and a man with a red cap, and another pirate, dart below through one of the deck hatches. It was almost dark and a thick fog was swirling in from the sea. If I was going to find Ben Gunn's boat I had no time to waste.

It took me an hour to crawl through thick scrub to the base of the white rock. Sure enough, I found a little tent made of goatskins hidden in some bushes. I opened a flap in the tent which served as a door. There was the home-made boat Ben Gunn had described. I'd never seen a scrappier construction in my life. It was similar to a *coracle*, a craft made of sticks and hides that ancient fishermen once used. But it was so small and roughly assembled, I could hardly believe it would float with a full-sized man sitting inside it.

I crouched by the boat for a while, my mind suddenly racing with plots and schemes. All I'd planned on doing was to see if the boat existed and then report back to my captain. But a new idea now gripped me: I could row out to the *Hispaniola* under cover of darkness and fog, then cut her adrift so she would run aground and be ruined. It would be a terrible blow for our enemy to lose their ship and I thought I could accomplish it easily.

I waited for nightfall to steal over the island, then lifted the coracle onto my shoulders and hurried down to the breaking surf.

I discovered immediately that the coracle was a safe and sturdy craft, although almost impossible to steer. Ben Gunn had described her as *hard to handle*, and I kept repeating this phrase to myself as she whirled around in circles and drifted in every direction except the one I wanted. As luck would have it, the tide carried me towards the blinking lights of the *Hispaniola* and I was soon bobbing under her anchor cable. I grabbed hold and was surprised at how tightly stretched the line was. All around the ship the water currents bubbled and chattered like little mountain streams. The tide was already so strong it was dragging the ship on her anchor. One cut with my sailor's knife would send her racing away.

I didn't want to hack into the thick rope of the cable when it was so taut - I remembered an old sailor telling me that when a cable snaps it can be as dangerous as a kicking horse. So, I decided to wait for a gust of wind to turn the ship momentarily out of the rushing water. When I heard the sails creaking and felt the cable go slack in the water, I seized my chance and began sawing through the twisted strands of rope - until there were only two still holding the ship in place. I would cut through these when the wind came up again, giving me time to escape before the pirates noticed the ship was drifting loose.

All the time I'd been gripping the cable, I'd been aware of two voices arguing in the cabin. As I sat poised to cut through the last strands of rope, I recognized one of the men from his voice - it was Israel Hands. He was in a rage, and I guessed he'd been at the rum. This was confirmed when I saw a porthole crash open above me and an arm flicking an empty bottle into the sea.

The voices grew louder until I was sure the men were going to start brawling. Suddenly the wind changed again and I heard another voice ringing across the waves, coming from the island:

"But one man of her crew alive.
What put to sea with seventy-five."

It was a lone pirate in the swamp, singing the tune I'd heard so many times on the voyage to Treasure Island, never guessing how horribly appropriate it would turn out to be. Feeling the cable go slack again, I sliced through the two remaining strands.

The ship lurched on the tide, almost swamping my tiny coracle. As I desperately pushed my way along the side of the ship, I felt something brush my fingertips. It was a rope trailing down from the ship's deck.

I grasped it, not really knowing what I was doing, but too intrigued by this unexpected opportunity to let go. A few feet above me, I could see the open porthole to the main cabin. I hauled myself up to a standing position in the coracle, longing to have a peek inside the ship. We were rushing along on the current by now, but there were no shouts of alarm from the two sailors. What had happened to them, I wondered? One glance over the rim of the porthole told me everything I needed to know.

Hands and the other sailor were locked together in deadly combat, red-faced and furious, each with a hand at the other's throat. I dropped down into the coracle, ready to make an immediate escape, but the next instant the ship rolled violently and seemed to pick up speed, throwing me off balance. We had changed course, and my heart was in my mouth when I realized what I'd done.

The *Hispaniola* was rushing towards the narrow inlet at the end of Skeleton Island. She would be broken to pieces on the raging breakers, or lost on the open sea - and I was being pulled along with her.

There was a shout from inside the ship and the sound of running feet. But I was too frozen with fear to glance up at the deck to see what was happening. Then the coracle suddenly dropped away from the ship. I curled up in a ball in my craft of sticks and skins, trying not to think of the mighty, crashing ocean ahead of me. For hours, I was thrown about on huge waves, expecting certain death with every plunge, until sleep rescued me at last. I lay in my sea-tossed coracle, dreaming of home and life at the dear, old, *Admiral Benbow*.

I woke in daylight, drenched and weary after a night on the water. When I'd rubbed my eyes clear of sea spray I saw that I was only a quarter of a mile off land, at the south-west end of Treasure Island. At first, I thought I could paddle to shore, but then I saw the breakers grinding away at the cliffs and realized I'd be killed if I came in any closer. There were other dangers along that strip of great boulders and cliffs: sea monsters. Blinking my eyes, I saw around forty, slithering beasts crawling around on the rocks, bellowing and barking like massive snails out of their shells. I decided I would rather starve at sea before I came anywhere near them. (They were sea lions, Dr. Livesey has since told me, and not usually aggressive towards people.)

From what I remembered of Flint's map, I thought my best chance of finding a landing place was along the west coast of the island. Although I could do nothing to navigate the coracle, she seemed to be drifting with the current in the right direction. Ben Gunn's craft skimmed along, finding her way through great mounds of blue water and white foam.

I had hoped that the current would take me close enough to the Cape of Woods - as marked on the map - to attempt a landing. But, after several hours of drifting, I saw that I was still too far out to sea to use the paddle ,and was rapidly floating past the Cape. I might have given into despair if I hadn't seen a shining flash of white sails ahead of me - it was the *Hispaniola*. and she was coming straight for me.

"They must have sighted the coracle," I gasped.

But suddenly, I saw the ship turn out of the wind and roll about on the waves until the sails filled with wind. Then, after a minute or two of good sailing, she turned out of the breeze again. When I saw this repeated, time and time again, I guessed the cause: there was nobody steering her. Hands and the other man must have panicked as she rushed towards the channel in the darkness and deserted her. If this was the case, I might be able to board the ship. Perhaps I could even return the vessel to her rightful captain, Mr. Smollett?

I must have been half-mad with thirst, with the sun baking my head, but I started paddling desperately towards the drifting ship. It took me a good hour of hard work to get close to her, but finally she stopped on the waves only a hundred yards away. All her sails were limp and I could see the cabin windows and the lamp still burning from the night before. If I could only manage one last burst of paddling, I would catch her. But, while I was gathering all my strength for the challenge, I saw the sails billow and flap into life and she was off again.

I almost screamed in frustration - but then I almost screamed with joy. The *Hispaniola* had dipped and turned and suddenly her prow was slicing through the waves, rushing towards me. There was no time to think. I found myself riding on top of one wave, with the ship looming above me on the next. Springing to my feet, I made a wild leap for some ropes hanging from the bowsprit. As I caught hold of the line and swung my legs up, I heard a crunch as the coracle disappeared under the *Hispaniola's* hull.

I had made my choice, and there was no going back now.

The ship lurched and rolled on the sea as I tumbled onto the main deck. Every step was dangerous, but I didn't have to go far to discover the two pirate watchmen. Hands was lying on his back, propped up against the bulwarks with his arms across his chest. His face looked as white and greasy as candle wax and he lay in a pool of blood. The other man was in a worse condition: he was stretched out on the deck, as stiff as a plank and with his lips drawn back over his teeth in a horrible grimace. The two men must have rekindled their argument during the night and fought to the death.

While I studied their bodies, the ship kept bucking and rolling like a vicious stallion. The long wooden beam had broken loose and was swaying over the decks like a pendulum. "I was safer on the coracle," I muttered to myself.

At this, Hands groaned and his whole body twisted in pain. "Brandy," he hissed, and I saw his eyes roll open.

I hadn't forgotten that it was Hands who had tried to blow my friends out of the water with the cannon, but I still couldn't stand about and watch him suffer. Gripping the bulwarks and handrails, I carefully made my way down to the cabin. The scene below decks was incredible: every cupboard and chest had been forced open and the walls were covered in grubby handprints, evidence of the pirates' frantic search for the treasure map. Empty bottles rolled across the floor. From the number of them, I guessed Flint's crew had been drunk since we'd reached the island.

After foraging in the hold, I dug out a brandy bottle and some food for my aching stomach - cheese, pickled fruits and dry biscuits - before returning to the deck. I took a long drink of cool water from the water beaker and gave Hands his bottle. He'd swigged a good third of it before he set it down on the deck.

"I needed that," he growled in satisfaction.

"Are you badly hurt?" I asked him, munching away at my supplies.

"If the doctor was here, I'd be well in no time," he barked. "That's me, Jim, always unlucky. But that swab over there's unluckier still," he said, nodding his head to the other man. "He's good and dead. Now tell me, where did you spring from?"

"I'm taking control of the ship," I said proudly. "You can call me captain, Mr. Hands."

Then I walked over to the main mast and lowered the Jolly Roger. "We can't have that flag, can we?" I said, tossing it overboard.

"Well, captain," said Hands, "I suppose you'll want to try sailing the ship now, won't you?"

"Of course," I replied.

"You won't get far without my help though, will you?" he added craftily. "But if you fetch me food, drink and bandages for my wounds, I'll teach you how to sail her. I call that a deal, don't you, captain?"

I had no choice but to accept his offer. When I told him my plan was to find a deserted spot on the north shore where I could beach the ship, he only grunted. "I'm in no position to argue, am I?" he joked, pointing to the blood-splattered deck around him.

I found him some food and a silk handkerchief to bind a deep gash in his thigh. Then he instructed me on how to fix the sails and steer the ship into the wind. In no time at all we were flying around the rough, northern coast of the island, with the sea glittering in the sun. Hands had pulled himself up so his back was against the tiller. He studied me as I went about my tasks on the deck, an odd smile playing across his lips. It was an old man's smile, weak and resigned to his fate. But now and again, I saw a flash of cunning, a shadow of treachery as he watched my every move.

"This is an unlucky ship, captain," Hands called to

me suddenly. "So many dead sailors in her since we left Bristol. You're an educated boy," he grinned. "Look at this dead man here. Do you think he's gone for good, or can he live again?"

"You can't kill a man's spirit," I answered boldly. "The man you killed might be watching us from another world."

"If that's so," Hands chuckled, "it's a waste of my time killing anyone. But I don't think too much of spirits. I'll take my chances with them." He licked his lips. "Will you pop below and get me some wine, Jim? This brandy's too strong for me. Makes me dizzy."

It was obvious to me that Hands was plotting something. I'd already seen him glugging brandy as though it was water. But I decided to play along and find out what he was up to.

"I'll have to dig around for it," I told him, and hurried below. But, as soon as I was in the cabin, I slipped off my shoes and ran silently along the corridor to the forecastle hatch. When I popped my head out into the daylight, I could see Hands dragging himself across the deck, unaware that I was spying on him. He stopped at a coil of rope and picked out a long knife with a jagged edge, red to the hilt with blood. I watched him test the point of the knife on his palm, smile with satisfaction and then hide the weapon in his jacket. He glanced around and then crawled back to his old place against the tiller.

The thought of Hands lunging at me with that blood-smeared knife made me shiver, but I guessed that he was just as anxious to beach the ship as I was.

My life would be safe until we were on dry land. Doing my best to hide my thoughts, I returned to the cabin, found a bottle and climbed the stairs to the deck.

The rogue pretended he was dozing until I was next to him, then smiled and snapped the head off the wine bottle as though he'd done it a thousand times. "Here's luck," he growled, taking a swig. "I'm not long for this world, Jim. I can feel my end coming."

"Then say a prayer, Mr. Hands," I replied angrily, thinking of the knife under his shirt.

"I'm not the praying kind," he snapped. "For thirty years I've sailed the seas, seen good times and bad, fair weather and foul. I've witnessed starvation, thirst and bloodshed. But I've never seen anything good come of goodness. Strike first, I say. Dead men don't bite. That's the best way to go about things. Now, let's take this ship in."

We were only two miles from the island, and for the next hour we carefully navigated our way into the small bay of the North Inlet. Once we were inside, land closed in around us and I could see the thick forest of Treasure Island flashing by on either side of the ship.

"We're not the first," barked Hands. Only a mile ahead of us, I spotted an old ship beached on a narrow strip of sand. She was a wreck, covered in seaweed and forest creepers after rotting for years in this lonely backwater. "We can pull up next to that one," he cried.

"But how will we get her off again?" I asked him.

"Fix a rope and pulley to a tree and heave-ho," he laughed. "Now bring in that sail."

He had me running all over the deck with his commands, until we were hurtling towards the beach. I could hear the ship hissing through the shallow water, and in my excitement to watch, I rushed over to the bulwarks and leaned over the side.

I can't say exactly what it was that saved my life. Perhaps I heard a creak, or saw a shadow flicker across the rushing waves? But suddenly I jumped around and saw Hands looming over me with his knife held high. He roared like a charging bull and threw himself at my chest. But his wounds made him clumsy and weak and I sidestepped him easily, backing away on the deck and drawing one of my pistols. I took careful aim and pulled the trigger - the hammer clicked shut, but nothing happened.

"Your powder's wet," Hands growled at me, lumbering across the planks. "And you've nowhere to run."

He tried to lunge at me again, but I dodged around the main mast. Like two children chasing each other around a chair, we stumbled around the thick pillar of wood. The next second, the *Hispaniola* crashed onto the beach, throwing Hands and me across the deck. We slammed into the bulwarks as the ship rolled onto her side, and Hands would have caught me if it hadn't been for the dead sailor. His corpse tumbled after us and pinned Hands to the boards.

I struggled to my feet and tried to climb the sloping deck. But it was so slippery with seawater and grime that it was impossible to make any progress. When I saw Hands wriggle out from under the corpse and strike at me, I knew I had to find another escape route. There was a rope dangling over my head. I scrambled up into the rigging, dragging myself up the mast until I found a perch on a cross bar, thirty feet above the deck.

Hands stared up at me, cursing his bad luck as I set about reloading my pistols. He fixed the long knife between his lips and started hauling himself up the mast, groaning with pain each time he moved his injured leg.

"One more step, Mr. Hands," I called down to him, "and I'll blow your brains out." I had both pistols ready, aimed straight at his forehead, only ten feet below me. "Dead men don't bite, you know," I added, with a chuckle.

Hands slipped the dagger from his lips so he could speak. "Jim," he said softly, "let's sign a declaration of peace. I tried my best to catch you, but like I said, I'm unlucky. Let's strike a deal."

I was feeling so triumphant and sure of myself, I hardly noticed his hand reaching back over his shoulder. Something sang through the air like an arrow and I felt a sharp sting of pain. I was pinned to the mast with his knife through my shoulder. My body must have shuddered with the shock, as both my pistols exploded and I watched Hands fall head first into the water. The old pirate broke the surface in a lather of blood and foam and then sank to the bottom for good.

When the water settled, I could see his body stretched out on the bright sand of the shallows. He was shot and drowned, food for the fishes in the very place he'd planned to slaughter me.

In the Pirates' Den

I came to feeling sick and terrified, with hot blood streaming over my back and chest. The knife seemed to burn my skin like a branding iron and my first thought was to try to pluck it out of my shoulder. As I twisted my body to reach for it, I shuddered violently in pain and the blade broke free. The knife, it turned out, had only held me to the mast by a pinch of skin above my shoulder. With the blood running even faster, I breathed a sigh of relief that Hands' missile had missed the bone.

I dropped down to the deck and managed to find some cloth to bandage the wound. Once this was done, I decided to clear the ship of the dead pirate. I was feeling so bold by this stage, I bundled him over the side as though he'd been an unwanted sack of coal. He went to join the man who had killed him at the bottom of the bay.

By the time I'd lowered all the ship's sails - to stop her from being blown around on any high winds - the tide had gone out and the whole inlet was bathed in twilight. I waded ashore and marched into the woods, anxious to get back to my friends and boast of capturing the ship. It was still only dusk, and I thought I had a good idea of the lay of the land. But I was soon tripping into bushes and rolling into shallow pits, trying to pick my way through the darkening woods. When the moon came up I made better progress, and my legs were still strong when I found myself next to the wooden stakes of the stockade.

My greatest fear was being shot by my own friends, mistaking me for an intruder, so I scaled the fence silently and tiptoed up to the blockhouse. I was surprised to see the glowing embers of a fire out in the middle of the enclosure, knowing that Captain Smollett wanted to conserve our firewood. But then I heard something that put my mind at rest: loud snoring, coming from inside the log cabin. I had complained about it in the past, but that noise was sweet music to my ears after so long away.

With my arms reaching out into the darkness, I took a step into the blockhouse. I planned to lie down in my old place and let them find me in the morning, and was already looking forward to seeing their amazed expressions when they heard my story.

There was a sudden rustle, a sound like pecking, then a screech: "Pieces of eight, pieces of eight."

"Who goes there?" roared Long John Silver, roused by his parrot. I turned to run but an arm snaked out and held my wrist in a steel grip.

"Fetch a torch," cried Silver. "Let's see who's come visiting."

The red glare of the torch showed me everything I most feared: the pirates had taken the fort and there were no signs of any prisoners. My friends had all died: I had abandoned them when they needed me most.

Silver had a crew of six pirates in all. One of them was badly injured, and I recognized the man who had been shot in the first attack and had fled into the woods. The other five were still drunk from a night of debauchery. Only Silver was sober, and I thought he looked pale and stern compared to his usual self. He was still dressed in his fine clothes, but they were worn now, smeared with mud and clay, torn on the sharp thorns of the woods.

"Shiver my timbers," he cried, when the torch was lifted close to my face. "Have you decided to join us, Jim Hawkins? Quite a pleasant surprise for old John. I knew you were a smart one when I first saw you, but this strategy of yours is a mystery, even for me."

He slumped down onto a cask and began filling his pipe, while the other pirates circled around me, glowering and muttering oaths.

"I've always liked you, Jim," Silver continued. "You remind me of myself when I was young and handsome. So, I'm glad you've come to join our company. The captain was very disappointed when you deserted, and the doctor called you an *ungrateful scamp*, but you're very welcome on our side, Jim. We won't turn you away. Are you with us then?"

So at least my friends were still alive, even if they were furious with me for running off.

"But what's happened here," I cried.

"The doctor came to us yesterday," Silver explained, "with a flag of truce. When we saw the ship was gone, there was nothing to do but make a bargain. We got the fort and all the supplies, in return for letting them march off into the forest, unharmed. You weren't mentioned in the deal, but they did say they were sick of you disappearing, wandering off when they needed you. Now make your choice. Are you with us?"

"I might be a fool," I shouted, suddenly losing my temper with Silver and his band of killers, "but I'm not a big enough fool to sign up with the likes of you. And, if we're setting the record straight, you might as well know the whole truth. It was me who took Billy Bones' map, me who heard you plotting and warned the captain. And it was me who cut the ship's cable, killed your guards and hijacked her. You'll never see her again. I've outsmarted you from the beginning, and I don't care if you kill me or not. All I'll say is that if you spare me now, I'll remember this one good deed and do my best to save your lives from the rope when you finally stand trial for mutiny in England."

They stared at me in dumbstruck amazement for a few seconds, then one of them drew a long knife and rushed at me. "I'll deal with this scamp," he cried.

"Steady on there, Tom Morgan," roared Silver, leaning forward from his seat on the barrel and holding my attacker back. "Who made you captain here? Cross me and I'll send you to hell, man."

"Tom's right," called one of the pirates.

"We're tired of you giving the orders, Barbecue," cried another.

"You dare challenge me?" roared Silver, stretching himself up to his full height. "Let's see one of you pick up a cutlass, and we'll see his insides spill out."

Not one of them moved.

"If you won't fight me," Silver snarled, "you'll obey me. And I say nobody touches this boy."

My heart was beating like a sledgehammer in the silence that followed, while Silver crossed his arms and smoked his pipe as calmly as a man standing at a church meeting. Slowly, the other pirates fell back into a huddle in the far corner of the blockhouse, where I heard them whispering.

"If you've got something to say," remarked Silver, "let me hear it too."

"This crew's got rights," spat one of the men from the huddle, "and we're stepping outside to hold a council."

One by one, the men filed out of the blockhouse, each giving Silver a formal salute as they disappeared into the night. The instant they had gone, Silver was whispering urgently in my ear: "Jim, you're only a half-plank away from death, and maybe torture too. They're going to sack me, I reckon, but I'll do everything I can to save you. From now on, Jim, we're in this together, fighting back to back for our lives. Will you be my witness in court, Jim, like you said you would?"

"I'll do what I can for you," I replied, hardly believing that my former enemy was now my best ally.

"I'm on the squire's side again, Jim," said Silver with a chuckle, helping himself to a cup of brandy. "I know you've got the ship hidden somewhere safe and I know when I'm beaten. But what still puzzles me, lad, is why did the doctor give me Flint's map? Do you know the answer to that riddle, Jim?"

But I could only shake my head and watch him gulping at his brandy, like a man who is expecting the worst.

The six pirates returned in solemn silence. They pushed one man forward as their spokesperson. He stepped nervously towards Silver, holding his clenched fist in front of him.

"There's no need for that, lad," Silver boomed. "I know the rules and I won't harm the messenger."

The sailor passed something to Silver and hurried back to his friends.

"The black spot," hissed Silver, staring into his palm. "But where did you get the paper? This is bible paper."

"What did I tell you?" snapped Morgan to the other pirates. "I said no good would come of using a bible."

"You're all cursed now," purred Silver. "You're gallows meat."

"Enough talking," shouted a tall pirate. "This crew's given you the black spot. Do your duty, turn it over and see what's written there."

"Deposed," growled Silver, reading from the paper. "Well, let's hear your grievances. I'm still captain until I've had the chance to answer them."

"You've made a hash of this cruise," said the tall pirate. "You let the enemy out of this trap for nothing and you wouldn't let us attack them on their march through the woods. And, last of all, there's this business with the boy."

"By the powers!" cried Silver. "It wasn't me who

scuppered this cruise. If I'd had my way, we'd have stayed with the ship, and waited for the squire to *take* us to the treasure. It was your own impatience that sank us. Do you know how close we are to hanging? Have you seen the birds flapping round the buccaneers' corpses on Execution Dock, their chains jangling in the wind? We're all due to hang and dry like that in the sun, because you rushed me, pestered me, from the moment we left Bristol."

I could see some of the pirates frowning, muttering to one another as Silver's words sank in. He wiped the sweat from his brow - his whole body had been shaking with rage during the speech - then continued.

"And you want to know about the boy? Well, have you ever heard of a hostage, you poor swabs? I won't let you fools kill our only hostage."

"Why did you let the others go, then?" snarled the tall man.

"You were starving and diseased down in that swamp," cried Silver. "You begged me for food and first aid so I got them for you. And there's more."

With a sweep of his arm he dropped something onto the dirt floor. Even in the dim light of the blockhouse, I could see it was Flint's treasure map.

The pirates jumped on the map like cats after a mouse.

"It's Flint's!" cried one man, in an excited squeal. "I know his writing."

"But we've no ship," said another. "What good is this to us if we can't get the gold off the island?"

"Stop this," cried Silver. "It was you who lost me the ship. I found you the treasure and look at the thanks I'm given. Well, you can elect yourselves a new captain. I resign."

"Barbecue for captain," shouted one of them.

"Aye," said another. "We'll stick with Long John."

"I accept," roared Silver. "Jim, here's a keepsake for you."

He flicked the scrap of paper they'd given him towards me and I caught it in the air. It was size of a large coin, one side blackened with wood ash, the other featuring the single, scrawled word.

"Now we can drink," cried Silver, raising a cheer from the pirates. "And to treasure in the morning."

A Treasure Hunt

I woke to hear a pirate shouting at the door: "The doctor's here, Silver. Come to see his patients."

I ran to a gun slit and saw my old friend standing in the same place where Silver had waited with his white flag, waist-high in fog at the edge of the forest.

"Come in, sir," laughed Silver. "Come in for a chat. We've got quite a surprise for you this morning. We've got a new lodger, a little stranger, and fit as a fiddle he looks too."

"Jim?" the doctor gasped, stopping in his tracks. In a few seconds he had recovered his composure and ducked inside the doorway of the blockhouse. He gave me one, grim nod of acknowledgement and then hurried over to the injured pirate.

"You had a close shave," he told the man. "Your head must be as hard as iron."

Livesey's bravery was incredible. He moved among the men, checking them for fever and dispensing pills as though he was out on his country rounds. "Three men have the fever," he told Silver, when he had finished his work. "That's what comes of making camp in a bog. Now," he said casually, "I should like to talk with the boy."

The mood of the pirates changed in a flash. I saw one of them look up with hate in his eyes and cry: "Not one word."

"Silence," growled Silver. "We'll do this my way.

Jim, will you give me your word as a gentleman, you won't try to run away."

"I will."

"Then, doctor," said Silver, "I thank you for abiding by the treaty we made, and caring for my crew. In return for your kindness, if you'll wait on the other side of the stockade, I'll bring the boy down and you can talk between the stakes."

When the doctor was halfway down the hill, the pirates began screaming with fury at Silver. They accused him of treachery and double-dealing, and for a moment I thought Long John had lost control of them completely.

"This time I won't be rushed into violence," he bellowed over their heads. "I don't want the enemy to suspect we're leaving today to find the treasure, do I? Let me play the fox with our enemies. Now make a fire. We'll have a hearty breakfast when I get back."

We set off down the hill, leaving the pirates grumbling behind us. When we reached the doctor, Silver leaned forward and began talking quickly, making sure his face couldn't be observed from the blockhouse. "The boy will tell you how I saved his life," he whispered. "I risked everything to do it, and now I'm stranded between two ships. I don't want to hang, sir. Remember that I saved Jim, before you judge me. I'll give you a minute to speak in private."

He turned on his crutch and hobbled a few yards to a tree stump, where he sat whistling, watching both us and the scowling pirates waiting at the blockhouse.

"So, Jim," said the doctor sadly. "You've made your bed and now you must lie in it. I can't find it in my heart to blame you. But to run off when the captain was ill - that was downright cowardly."

When I heard this, I let out a sob and my cheeks ran with tears. "Forgive me, doctor. I'm sure to die because of what I've done, and would be dead already if Silver hadn't saved me. But I can bear dying. What I fear is being tortured..."

"I can't have this," spat the doctor in sudden outrage. "Over you come, Jim. We'll make a run for it."

"I gave my word, sir."

"I'll bear the shame of that, lad," he said softly. "Now jump, and we'll run like antelopes."

"You wouldn't break your word, sir," I replied. "Neither would the captain, or the squire, and neither can I. But, doctor, you didn't let me finish. I fear torture because I might let slip where I've hidden the ship."

"The ship?" he exclaimed.

I quickly told him about my adventure and the location of the *Hispaniola*. He listened to everything in silence, then paused before responding.

"You've saved our lives again," he said at last, tenderly. "We couldn't let you die, Jim."

At the corner of my eye I saw Silver approaching. "Time to go," he called out, loud enough so his pirate crew could hear him.

"Silver, I'll give you some advice," the doctor whispered. "Don't be in a hurry to go looking for that treasure."

"If I don't hurry," Long John answered, "I'm dead and so is Jim.'

"Then look out for squalls and thunder when you find it," said the doctor mysteriously. "Keep the boy beside you at all times, and shout for help when you need it most. If you get Jim out of this wolf trap alive, I'll do my best to save you in court." Dr. Livesey shook hands with me through a gap in the stockade, nodded to Silver and darted off into the forest.

"Jim, I owe you my life," hissed Silver, as we climbed the hill to the blockhouse. "I can hear a pin drop on a ship's deck, and I heard the doctor ask you to jump the fence. If you'd gone, my men would have made short work of me. We're square now, in it together, off on a strange voyage. But courage, lad, we'll sail on through."

We left the camp an hour later, each one of the six buccaneers loaded down with picks, guns and supplies. Silver made it clear that I was their prisoner, and not to be trusted outside the camp. He tied a rope around my middle and led me along like a dancing bear.

We took to the boats and rowed for an hour, landing in the forest at the foot of Spyglass Hill. Silver consulted the map and had the men scour the terrain for the *tall tree*, mentioned by Flint as a marker.

"There are dozens of them on that high plateau," complained one of the pirates. "How can we tell which one it is?"

"We'll climb up there," replied Silver. "Gold doesn't come easy, mates."

It was a beautiful, fresh day, and we made good progress through thickets of green nutmeg trees and lush meadows dotted with wild flowers. But the going was hard for Silver, and we were struggling to keep up with the group when we heard a cry of terror, echoing down the hillside.

"It can't be the treasure," gasped Morgan, breaking into a run. "What can it be, Silver?"

When we reached the man who'd given the shout, we saw something that made every man shudder. Stretched out at the base of a tall pine tree was a skeleton, still dressed in some shreds of cloth - sailor's cloth.

"He's a seaman," gasped one of the pirates.

"You wouldn't find a bishop lying there, would you," said Silver cruelly. "But, shipmates, don't you think there's something odd about the position of the bones?"

When I looked closely, I saw that the man had his arms arranged above his head, pointing in a straight line.

"It's a pointer," hissed Silver suddenly. "Old Flint has left us a clue. It's one of his jokes, I'll bet, to leave one of the men he killed up here as a compass. But shiver my timbers! Those are long bones, and the hair on the skull's yellow."

"It's Allardyce," cried Morgan. "He owed me money, the day Flint took him to shore."

"It's creepy," whispered Silver. "These dry bones pointing towards the treasure. There were six of them, that day, and there are six of you now."

"But Flint's dead," barked Morgan. "Remember, we put pennies on his eyes."

"He might be dead," said the man with the bandaged head, "but who'd make a better ghost than bad old Flint?"

"He raged and screamed for rum all his life," said another man. "And he was always singing his song, *Fifteen Men*. I heard it the day he died, coming out of his open porthole in the death chamber."

"Let's get moving," growled Silver defiantly. "Flint's gone, boys, and I want those doubloons."

We started up the hill again, but I noticed the pirates stayed in a tighter group than before. The fear of their dead captain was still alive in their minds.

We came out on a plateau covered with low woods and the men fell down in some long grass to rest.

"I can see the tall trees ahead of us, lads," said Silver cheerfully.

But the others were gloomy and quiet. When they did say something, it was almost in a whisper. All of a sudden, a thin, trembling voice from deep in the woods started singing that familiar melody:

> *"Fifteen men on the dead man's chest -*
> *Yo-ho-ho and a bottle of rum!"*

The pirates screamed, clawed at the ground or jumped to their feet in alarm. As suddenly as it had started, the phantom singing stopped dead on a last echoing note.

"It's Flint," cried Morgan.

"It's only a prank," replied Silver, struggling to get the words out without his voice shaking. He tried to calm the men with a weak laugh, but he was interrupted by the same, haunting voice sounding from the woods.

"Fetch me my rum, Darby McGraw," the voice commanded.

"His last words," moaned Morgan. "Only his ghost could know those."

I could hear Silver's teeth rattling with fright, but he clamped them together, refusing to give in to his fear. "I've come for the treasure," he cried, "and no man or devil is going to stop me. I'll shake my fist in this ghost's face, for all that gold."

But the men were too terrified to answer their captain. They formed a circle in the clearing, staring into the black woods.

"There was an echo to that voice," Silver barked suddenly. "Ghosts don't throw shadows and they don't make echoes."

To my amazement, the other pirates took comfort from this explanation.

"You're right, John," whispered the bandaged man. "And come to think of it, that voice is *like* Flint's but it reminds me of someone else?"

"Ben Gunn," roared Silver.

"That was it," cried Morgan. "But what's he doing here?"

"Dead or alive, I don't fear Ben Gunn," Silver shouted. "Ben Gunn wouldn't harm a fly."

The next instant the pirates were picking up their loads and smiling to one another. They were back on the treasure hunt - keener than ever.

We crossed the plateau and made our way towards a line of three, huge trees poking out of the scrub. The first proved to be on a different compass bearing from the one described on the map. But when we checked the position of the second tree - a giant redwood almost two hundred feet tall - Silver let out a cry that chilled my blood. He yanked on my rope as he hurried forwards, turning around to give me an awful scowl. Suddenly, he was a buccaneer again, his brain in a fever to be so close to Flint's gold. His crew ran ahead of us, baying like excited hounds. The next instant, we heard a shout ahead of us, and Silver pushed his way through the bushes at the base of the tree.

I looked down and saw a great pit in the earth, littered with broken picks and rotting boards from old packing cases. There was grass sprouting at the bottom

of the pit, and a plank of wood with the single word -
Walrus - scorched into it with a hot iron.

But there was no sign of Flint's treasure. It was all
gone - probably plundered long before.

The Captain Vanishes

"Stand by for trouble," whispered Silver, passing me a pistol. He led me around the pit so we were facing the six, stunned buccaneers arranged along the other side.

"We've been robbed, lads," cried Morgan. "Long John's led us on a wasted journey."

"He must have known all along," snarled the tall pirate. "He's gone in with the enemy, mates. There's only two of them, that old cripple and a scamp. Let's finish them off."

I saw the pirates reaching for their pistols. But, before they could draw and shoot, I heard the crack of musket shots exploding all around us. Three pirates lurched forwards into the pit; the others ran with all their speed towards the shelter of the woods.

When I turned around I saw the doctor, Gray and Ben Gunn hurrying towards us, smoke still pouring from their musket barrels.

"It's a race for the boats, lads," shouted the doctor, leading us in a sprint towards the plateau. Silver tried to keep up, but he was soon bellowing like an elephant with the effort. When I heard him shout, he seemed delighted: "There's no hurry, doctor, I see them."

The three mutineers were running for their lives, deeper into the heart of the island. We sat down to catch our breaths.

"Doctor, you came in the nick of time," gasped Silver when he'd joined us. "And it was you singing out in the woods, Ben Gunn. To think, Ben Gunn outwitted me."

"He was the hero," interrupted the doctor, "from beginning to end," and he outlined the story of the castaway as we strolled down to the sea.

In his long, lonely wanderings, Ben Gunn had stumbled across the skeleton and discovered the route to the treasure. It had taken him weeks of hard work to unearth the gold and carry it, piece by piece, to his cave in the forest.

When the doctor had heard this secret, he knew the map was worthless. So he had used it as a bargaining tool with Silver. Ben Gunn's cave was well-provisioned with all the fruits of the island, and if the party hid there they could guard the loot while the captain recovered from his wounds.

When the doctor realized I was a prisoner of the pirates, he ran back to the cave and fetched Gray and Ben Gunn with their rifles, leaving the squire to protect the captain. It had been Ben Gunn's idea to terrify the pirates by mimicking Flint's voice, to give the doctor and Gray time to catch up with them.

We took one of the boats and smashed the other into tiny pieces. Then we set off on the long row to the North Inlet of the island, where we found the *Hispaniola* drifting free of the sand bar. A high tide and strong winds had lifted her off. We quickly fixed a new anchor to her, leaving Gray to stand guard on the deck that evening.

Next, we rowed around to Rum Cove, the closest beach to Ben Gunn's treasure cave. The squire greeted me with a warm smile, and said nothing about my desertion. I hoped that the return of the ship had been enough to make him forgive me.

But when Silver rushed over and made a salute, Trelawney bristled: "John Silver, you're an irredeemable villain, sir," he cried. "But I have been asked by my friends not to prosecute you. Very well. You are safe. Let your conscience punish you, and the memory of all the dead men who hang about your neck like millstones."

"Thank you kindly, sir," replied Silver, with a smirk.

We entered the cave, a large, airy cavern with a little spring of clear water. Captain Smollett was resting by a small fire, but my eyes were drawn to a far corner of the cave, where a great pile of coins and bars of gold

flickered in the gloom. Seventeen men from the *Hispaniola* had died trying to recover this treasure. I tried, for one moment, to imagine all the horrors, sorrows and pains that had gone into collecting it. But it was too much for me to comprehend, so I turned back to my friends, and joined them in a hearty dinner of goat meat and fine red wine.

Silver lingered at the edge of our group, springing forward, like a steward, when anything was wanted. He was the same polite, fawning seaman as he had been before the mutiny.

I spent the next three days filling sacks with gold, while the others slowly ferried it out to the *Hispaniola*. It was a strange mass of coins, as tall as I was and as diverse as the pile I'd found in Billy Bones' chest. Almost every variety of money in the world was present in that huge hoard, I believe, and my fingers were soon aching with all the sorting.

On the evening before we left, we heard the three pirates crashing about in the swamp - they were either drunk or raving mad with fever. We'd been careful to post guards at all times, but they'd left us alone at Rum Cove. Perhaps they were hoping this truce would make us take pity on them? If so, they were mistaken.

We left them food, tools, musket powder and tobacco. But, on the fourth morning, we sailed out of the channel, marooning them on Treasure Island. I will never forget their screams for mercy, as they ran down to the beach, waving at the ship. But we couldn't risk another mutiny.

"They'll only hang if we take them home," snapped the captain, ignoring their desperate calls.

After ten days of storms and hard sailing, we reached the nearest port in Spanish America, where we hoped to find fresh hands for the voyage home. The contrast between this happy, noisy town and the brooding menace of Treasure Island lifted our spirits instantly. I wandered through the streets with the squire and the doctor, sampling the local fruits and laughing with the tradesmen. We soon encountered a Royal Navy captain, and passed the night as guests in his luxurious state rooms.

It was dawn before we returned to the *Hispaniola*, to find Ben Gunn waving his arms and begging us to forgive him. He had helped Silver to escape.

"I've saved your lives, sirs," he pleaded. "He's like a curse, the man with one leg. None of us would have lived to see England if he'd sailed with us."

Silver hadn't gone empty-handed - he'd snatched a sack of coins to help him on his wanderings. I think we were all pleased to be rid of him so cheaply.

The *Hispaniola* reached Bristol safely, with only five survivors from her original crew. We all received a fair share of the treasure. Captain Smollett retired from the sea with his fortune, while Gray studied to become a mate. He is now the co-owner of a cargo ship, and a contented family man. Ben Gunn had a thousand pounds, and spent it in twenty days. The squire gave him a job on his estate, and you can always hear the old castaway singing in church on Sundays.

Long John was gone for good. I hoped he was living in comfort somewhere, with his wife and Captain Flint. I wished him no harm, because his chances for happiness in the next world are so very small.

Some silver bars and scattered jewels still lie buried on the island. But wild horses couldn't drag me back to that place of horrors. In my nightmares, I can still hear the surf roaring along the island's coast and the voice of Captain Flint ringing like a scream:

"Pieces of eight, pieces of eight."

About
Robert Louis Stevenson

When Stevenson wrote *Treasure Island*, he must have doubted that he'd ever visit an island so exotic or far-flung as the one featured in his story. In his day, travel was still an expensive and arduous business, and Stevenson was a frail, sickly man. But his own life turned out to be more adventurous than any of his writings. Against all expectations, Stevenson spent his last years in a tropical paradise every bit as exciting as his literary creation.

Born in Edinburgh, in Scotland, in 1850, he always felt a passion for the wild landscapes of his homeland. In several of his books - notably *Kidnapped* (published in 1886) - he uses real locations for his fictional sword fights, shipwrecks and mountain chases. Scottish history fascinated him and provided him with the plots for many of his stories. But, although the country fuelled and excited his literary imagination, it ruined his health. Edinburgh was cold and damp for much of the year, and the climate had wrecked his lungs by the time he was three. For the rest of his life he suffered from breathlessness and violent fevers, and in the rare portraits that still exist Stevenson looks pale and pained.

His career as a writer took some time to get off the ground. Stevenson's father and grandfather were civil engineers who'd helped to build lighthouses around Scotland's rocky shores. They were anxious for young Robert Louis to preserve the family tradition, so he trained for several years as an engineer at Edinburgh University. But, when it became clear his health would never allow him to work outdoors, he changed his studies to law, qualifying as a barrister in 1875.

But Stevenson had no desire to follow a legal career. His one childhood love had been storytelling and, in 1878, he published his first book, a comic travelogue called *An Inland Voyage*. He worked hard, submitting reviews, essays and short stories to book publishers and magazines. Gradually, he got some of his work accepted. At a writers' retreat, he met Fanny Osbourne, an American ten years his senior. Fanny made quite an impression on him, and within two years they were married and honeymooning in an abandoned silver mine outside San Francisco.

This wasn't as strange as it might seem. Stevenson loved an adventure, he found the Californian climate good for his lungs, and his time in the wilderness gave him lots of material for his writing. The description of Treasure Island, for instance, owes more to America's fauna and flora than to any tropical habitat. Jim Hawkins talks of redwood trees and oaks, and tiptoes around a rattlesnake. None of these would be found on a tropical island, but must have been common in Stevenson's Californian hideaway. *Silverado Squatters*, his book about this experience, was published in 1883.

Back in Scotland, Stevenson and his new family struggled financially until the publication of *Treasure*

Island. After this, he produced a string of profitable books, including his famous *Dr. Jekyll and Mr. Hyde,* in 1886.

With his literary reputation blooming, and some money coming in at last, Stevenson listened to the advice of his doctors and returned to America. Fascinated by what he'd heard of the Pacific, he decided on a short voyage there with his mother, Fanny and her son Lloyd. In June 1888, they chartered the schooner *Casco* - not much smaller than the *Hispaniola* - from a Dr. Samuel Merrit. Merrit worried the writer might be *a kind of crank,* but warmed to him when they met. Stevenson hired the yacht for seven months and set sail. He would spend the rest of his life within the boundaries of the Pacific.

The long sea voyage did wonders for his health. He toured the Pacific islands, posting reports back to his publishers in London and New York. With the prospect of any return to Europe fading from his mind, Stevenson fell in love with the island of Upolu - now Western Samoa - and began putting down roots there in 1890. He built a house - Vailima - and enjoyed playing the role of the benevolent laird among the locals. They, in turn, were entertained by his efforts at farming and respected him as a writer, giving him the title *Tusitala* - storyteller. For four years, Stevenson lived and worked in his island paradise, on the opposite side of the world from the cottage where he'd begun *Treasure Island.* He died suddenly, on December 3, 1894, and was buried on a hillside overlooking the ocean.

Another Usborne Classic

Dr Jekyll & Mr Hyde

From the story by
Robert Louis Stevenson

Behind the locked door of Dr. Jekyll's laboratory lies a mystery his lawyer is determined to solve. Why does the doctor spend so much time there? What is the connection between the respectable Dr. Jekyll and his visitor, the loathsome Mr. Hyde? Why has Jekyll changed his will to Hyde's advantage? And who murdered Sir Danvers Carew?

This spine-chilling retelling brings Robert Louis Stevenson's classic horror story to life, and is guaranteed to thrill and terrify modern readers as much as when *The Strange Case of Dr. Jekyll and Mr. Hyde* was first published over a century ago.